JOHN WAYNE

★ ★ ★ ★ ★ ★ ★ ★ ★ ★ ★ ★ ★

POP CULTURE LEGENDS

JOHN WAYNE

★ ★

DON NARDO

CHELSEA HOUSE PUBLISHERS

New York ★ Philadelphia

CHELSEA HOUSE PUBLISHERS

EDITORIAL DIRECTOR Richard Rennert
EXECUTIVE MANAGING EDITOR Karyn Gullen Browne
COPY CHIEF Robin James
PICTURE EDITOR Adrian G. Allen
ART DIRECTOR Robert Mitchell
MANUFACTURING DIRECTOR Gerald Levine
ASSISTANT ART DIRECTOR Joan Ferrigno

Pop Culture Legends
SENIOR EDITOR Kathy Kuhtz Campbell
SERIES DESIGN Basia Niemczyc

Staff for JOHN WAYNE

EDITORIAL ASSISTANT Scott D. Briggs
DESIGN ASSISTANT Lydia Rivera
PICTURE RESEARCHER Ellen Barrett Dudley
COVER ILLUSTRATION Michael Hobbs

3 5 7 9 8 6 4

Library of Congress Cataloging-in-Publication Data

Nardo, Don.
John Wayne/Don Nardo.
p. cm.—(Pop culture legends)
Includes bibliographical references and index.
ISBN 0-7910-2348-6.
    0-7910-2373-7 (pbk.)
1. Wayne, John, 1907–1979—Juvenile literature. 2. Motion
picture actors and actresses—United States—Biography—Juvenile literature. [1. Wayne, John, 1907–1979. 2. Actors and
actresses.] I. Title. II. Series.
PN2287.W454N37 1994   94-17328
791.43'028'092—dc20   CIP
[B]   AC

FRONTISPIECE:

In *The Fighting Kentuckian,* released in 1949, John
Wayne plays a frontiersman who heroically clashes with
land-grabbing outlaws in 1810.

Contents ★ ★ ★ ★ ★ ★ ★ ★ ★ ★ ★ ★ ★ ★ ★ ★ ★ ★

A Reflection of Ourselves—*Leeza Gibbons*   7

★ **1**   A Big Man for the Big Trail   11

★ **2**   The Duke of Glendale   23

★ **3**   King of the Pecos   37

★ **4**   Reaping the Wild Wind of Fame   51

★ **5**   A New Monument in the Valley   65

★ **6**   Remembering the Alamo   79

★ **7**   An American Hero Versus the Two Big Cs   93

★ **8**   The Genuine Article   107

Appendix   118

Further Reading   123

Chronology   124

Index   126

A Reflection of Ourselves

Leeza Gibbons

I ENJOY A RARE PERSPECTIVE on the entertainment industry. From my window on popular culture, I can see all that sizzles and excites. I have interviewed legends who have left us, such as Bette Davis and Sammy Davis, Jr., and have brushed shoulders with the names who have caused a commotion with their sheer outrageousness, like Boy George and Madonna. Whether it's by nature or by design, pop icons generate interest, and I think they are a mirror of who we are at any given time.

Who are *your* heroes and heroines, the people you most admire? Outside of your own family and friends, to whom do you look for inspiration and guidance, as examples of the type of person you would like to be as an adult? How do we decide who will be the most popular and influential members of our society?

You may be surprised by your answers. According to recent polls, you will probably respond much differently than your parents or grandparents did to the same questions at the same age. Increasingly, world leaders such as Winston Churchill, John F. Kennedy, Franklin D. Roosevelt, and evangelist Billy Graham have been replaced by entertainers, athletes, and popular artists as the individuals whom young people most respect and admire. In surveys taken during each of the past 15 years, for example, General Norman Schwarzkopf was the only world leader chosen as the number-one hero among high school students. Other names on the elite list joined by General Schwarzkopf included Paula Abdul, Michael Jackson, Michael Jordan, Eddie Murphy, Burt Reynolds, and Sylvester Stallone.

More than 30 years have passed since Canadian sociologist Marshall McLuhan first taught us the huge impact that the electronic media has had on how we think, learn, and understand—as well as how we choose our heroes. In the 1960s, Pop artist Andy Warhol predicted that there would soon come a time when every American would be famous for 15 minutes. But if it is easier today to achieve Warhol's 15 minutes of fame, it is also much harder to hold on to it. Reputations are often ruined as quickly as they are made.

And yet, there remain those artists and performers who continue to inspire and instruct us in spite of changes in world events, media technology, or popular tastes. Even in a society as fickle and fast moving as our own, there are still those performers whose work and reputation endure, pop culture legends who inspire an almost religious devotion from their fans.

Why do the works and personalities of some artists continue to fascinate us while others are so quickly forgotten? What, if any, qualities do they share that enable them to have such power over our lives? There are no easy answers to these questions. The artists and entertainers profiled in this series often have little more in common than the enormous influence that each of them has had on our lives.

Some offer us an escape. Artists such as actress Marilyn Monroe, comedian Groucho Marx, and writer Stephen King have used glamour, humor, or fantasy to help us escape from our everyday lives. Others present us with images that are all too recognizable. The uncompromising realism of actor and director Charlie Chaplin and folk singer Bob Dylan challenges us to confront and change the things in our world that most disturb us.

Some offer us friendly, reassuring experiences. The work of animator Walt Disney and late-night talk show host Johnny Carson, for example, provides us with a sense of security and continuity in a changing world. Others shake us up. The best work of composer John Lennon and actor James Dean will always inspire their fans to question and reevaluate the world in which they live.

It is also hard to predict the kind of life that a pop culture legend will lead, or how he or she will react to fame. Popular singers Michael Jackson

and Prince carefully guard their personal lives from public view. Other performers, such as popular singer Madonna, enjoy putting their private lives before the public eye.

What these artists and entertainers do share, however, is the rare ability to capture and hold the public's imagination in a world dominated by mass media and disposable celebrity. In spite of their differences, each of them has somehow managed to achieve legendary status in a popular culture that values novelty and change.

The books in this series examine the lives and careers of these and other pop culture legends, and the society that places such great value on their work. Each book considers the extraordinary talent, the stubborn commitment, and the great personal sacrifice required to create work of enduring quality and influence in today's world.

As you read these books, ask yourself the following questions: How are the careers of these individuals shaped by their society? What role do they play in shaping the world? And what is it that so captivates us about their lives, their work, or the images they present?

Hopefully, by studying the lives and achievements of these pop culture legends, we will learn more about ourselves.

A Big Man for the Big Trail

O N A WARM DAY in the early autumn of 1929, veteran film director Raoul Walsh walked briskly across the lot of the Fox Film Corporation studio. Fox, located in the then sleepy little town of Hollywood on the outskirts of Los Angeles, California, was one of about a dozen large studios, or "majors," in America's popular and expanding movie industry. Walsh had earlier distinguished himself by directing many successful films, including the silent version of *The Thief of Bagdad* in 1924 and *In Old Arizona,* the first outdoor sound film, early in 1929. Now he was planning to shoot *The Big Trail,* an epic Western saga with a huge budget. The initial stages of preparation, called preproduction, had gone well except for one snag—he was having trouble finding a suitable leading man. He had approached two of the most popular actors of the day, Gary Cooper and Western star Tom Mix, but both were unavailable. The director's casting predicament was very much on his mind that afternoon as he made his way across the Fox lot.

Suddenly Walsh stopped in his tracks. A few yards away in front of a warehouse, a tall, well-built, and ruggedly handsome young man was in

---

John Wayne poses for a photograph while on location for *The Big Trail* in 1930. The tall and ruggedly handsome 22-year-old was a prop man when director Raoul Walsh chose him to play the crucial leading role in the sprawling Western.

the midst of unloading a truckful of furniture and other movie props. Walsh watched with fascination as the man easily lifted a sofa onto one shoulder, picked up a chair with his other hand, and carried them into the warehouse. The director's instinct and trained eye told him that this little-known laborer perfectly fit the part of Breck Coleman, *The Big Trail*'s male hero. Walsh recalled in his 1974 autobiography, *Each Man in His Time,* "When he came out for another load, I walked over and spoke to him."

Walsh learned that the young man's name was Marion Morrison but that most people called him Duke. Morrison told the director that he was 22 years old and was from the nearby town of Glendale, that he had attended the University of Southern California (USC) on a football scholarship, and that he was presently working as a prop man for the Fox studio. Was that his ambition—to become a prop man? Walsh inquired. Morrison confirmed that it was. When Walsh asked if he had had any acting experience, Morrison replied that in order to make some extra money he had done some bit parts, or small and mostly nonspeaking roles, for Fox and a few other studios. Without telling the young man the name of the film or any other details, Walsh told him to let his hair grow long for a couple of weeks, and then to report to the director's office for a screen test. Surprised and a bit perplexed, Morrison watched Walsh stride away.

True to his word, Walsh gave Morrison a screen test a few weeks later. Dressed in buckskin shirt and pants, the typical attire of Western movie heroes at the time, the nervous young man strutted around before a silent movie camera. Walsh then showed the footage to studio executive Winfield Sheehan. Sheehan liked the way Morrison looked and ordered a second test, this one with sound and including a few members of the film's supporting cast. Morrison still had no script to work with so he just ad-libbed some lines. Walsh and Sheehan were still impressed with him after the second test. But the studio was planning to sink a lot of money into the film and it seemed prudent to be as sure as possible that this untried young actor could handle the crucial lead role. So Morrison underwent a third test, this one with scripted lines and some of Walsh's expert coaching.

After some serious deliberation, Sheehan agreed with Walsh that Duke Morrison was the man for the part of Breck Coleman. But, as biographers Donald Shepherd and Robert Slatzer point out in their book *Duke: The Life and Times of John Wayne:*

> Sheehan, who made a practice of changing the names of his contract players, was dissatisfied with Duke's name. He thought Duke Morrison was a suitable name for a circuit preacher but not for a film actor. According to Walsh, the men retired to Sheehan's office, where the studio boss began jotting names on a note pad. None seemed suitable. While Sheehan continued writing, Walsh pulled a book about the Revolutionary War from a nearby shelf. As he leafed through it, the name Mad Anthony Wayne caught his eye. He showed it to Sheehan and the executive smiled. He liked the surname Wayne but rejected Anthony and so returned to his note pad, jotting down given names until he finally settled on the name John. John Wayne it was.

Thankful for getting this extraordinary break, the young actor did not object to being renamed. He knew that this was a standard practice in the film industry anyway.

Sheehan also considered how he was giving a newcomer, and a mere prop man at that, a lucky break. The executive took advantage of the fact by offering Wayne a salary of $75 per week, much less than most movie leads received at the time. Salaries of $500 to $1,000 per week were not uncommon and top stars like Tom Mix got as much as $5,000 per week. But in an era when one could rent a decent studio apartment for $3 or $4 per week and a complete dinner in a fine restaurant cost about a dollar, $75 per week was a lot of money for a young single man. So Wayne happily signed the contract.

The Big Trail was not scheduled to begin shooting for a few months and Walsh wisely used the time to prepare Wayne for his role. The director ordered veteran stuntman Jack Padgin to turn Wayne into a first-class cowboy. Padgin taught the young actor how to ride a horse, how to toss a lariat, and the proper use of rifles and handguns, while another stuntman, Steve Clemente, showed him how to throw a bowie knife. Wayne was an avid learner and a hard worker and before long he was able to handle himself like an authentic frontiersman.

In the spring of 1930, the cast and crew of the film assembled at the studio and prepared to depart for Yuma, Arizona, the first site of location shooting. Wayne was impressed by the huge mass of people and equipment and for the first time began to appreciate the true enormity and scope of the project he had become a part of. Set in the 1840s, the script depicted the adventures and hardships of a group of pioneers as they made their way by wagon train from Missouri to Oregon. Wayne's character, Breck Coleman, was the frontier scout who guided the settlers. The studio had spared no expense in making the project as large-scale, realistic, and authentic as possible. The film's budget was $2 million at a time when most Westerns cost between $10,000 and $75,000 to make.

Instead of being filmed in or near the studio, as most Westerns were at the time, *The Big Trail* was to be shot on locations spanning 2,000 miles of the American West. This required transporting, housing, and feeding a large crew, including 14 cameramen, 6 assistant directors, and dozens of lighting experts, makeup and costume people, animal handlers, and other specialized workers. Also part of the production's traveling company were 35 actors

with speaking parts and dozens of supporting extras. In addition, the studio had assembled more than 50 authentically re-created covered wagons, oxen to pull them, equally genuine costumes, rifles, and other props, as well as truckloads of lighting equipment, tents, wind machines, and portable dressing rooms.

In order to make the film even more impressive, the studio planned to shoot it in two distinct camera formats. The first, the then-standard 35-millimeter, which projected a small and roughly square screen image, would be suitable for most theaters in the country. The second format was a 55-millimeter process called Grandeur, a precursor of CinemaScope and other later wide-screen

Wayne's character, the frontier scout Breck Coleman, draws his knife to defend himself against a rival. *The Big Trail* tells the story of the first covered-wagon train to cross the Oregon Trail and of the ordeals the pioneers encountered on their dangerous trek west.

formats. This was intended for showing in specially equipped theaters in major cities. The trucks carrying the Grandeur equipment took their place in the company's enormous caravan of vehicles. Seeing the assembled company, Wayne realized, perhaps with a bit of apprehension, that the success of this expensive and ambitious venture depended to a considerable degree on how well he played his part. This made him more determined than ever to work as hard as possible.

Wayne's dedication paid off. When the cameras began rolling in Yuma, he impressed everyone in the company with his constant energy, serious attitude, and ability to take orders and direction. Walsh was especially pleased. As the company moved to Sacramento, California, to shoot scenes of the wagon train crossing rivers and on to Utah to get canyon vistas, the director increasingly felt that he had made the right decision in casting Wayne. According to Shepherd and Slatzer:

> Duke proved better in the role than Walsh had hoped. He was certainly the image of a frontier scout, and despite his youth, he had the imposing bearing, deep voice, and commanding presence of a leader of men. Walsh was especially impressed with his horsemanship, and he praised stuntman Jack Padgin, who was on location shooting as stunt coordinator, for a job well done in tutoring Duke. Duke handled a horse as though he had been riding all his life, and "his acting," Walsh wrote, "was instinctive, so that he became whatever and whomever he was playing."

A dramatic example of Wayne's instinctive acting ability occurred during the shooting of one of *The Big Trail*'s most spectacular scenes. While in Utah, Walsh shot a scene of the pioneers encountering a deep and impassable ravine with river rapids at the bottom. Although it was not in the script, the director decided to stage a sequence in which the settlers attempted to lower their wagons down the ravine's sheer wall. Jack Padgin and other stuntmen attached ropes to the wagons and livestock, and many of the actors and extras prepared to lower themselves down other ropes. Walsh yelled, "Action!" and the cameras began recording the exciting scene. Adding an unexpected touch of drama and realism, in the midst of the scene a wagon, luckily one with no one inside, suddenly slipped from its harness, hung in midair for several seconds, then plunged into the river. As these events unfolded, Wayne, as Coleman, rushed back and forth ad-libbing lines that perfectly fit the situation. Walsh later said, "I stood and watched him waving his arms and shouting orders and wondered where the youthful linebacker had gone. Instead of a football player, I had a star. . . . He was a natural."

After shooting several important scenes in Wyoming, *The Big Trail* wrapped, or finished shooting, and Wayne returned to California. There, he waited expectantly during postproduction, the filmmaking stage during which the final steps of editing and music scoring take place. When he saw the finished movie at a private showing at the studio, he and everyone else in the project were not disappointed. As Alan G. Barbour states in his biography of Wayne:

> The film turned out to be one of the most impressive and spectacular Westerns ever made. Highlights of the film included a realistically staged Indian attack on an encircled wagon train, an awe-inspiring buffalo hunt and chase, and panoramic displays of the pioneers encountering and overcoming natural hazards on their hazardous trek westward.

Wayne's performance in the film was solid and believable, especially striking for someone with so little acting experience, and he received many sincere compliments from members of both cast and crew. It appeared that the studio was preparing to promote him as a major new star. Wayne certainly believed this was the case when studio heads sent him on a publicity tour of midwestern and eastern cities. Attempting to familiarize the public with its leading man, Fox arranged several interviews for newspapers and magazines, among them a spread in *Photoplay* magazine. The interviewer, Miriam Hughes, was impressed with how modest and sincere Wayne was in comparison to many of Hollywood's conceited male stars. Wayne politely responded:

> I think I've got sense enough and that I've seen enough of the other kind to keep myself levelheaded. I've heard the

A panoramic scene from Raoul Walsh's *The Big Trail* shows authentically re-created covered wagons, Indian tepees, and costumes. Instead of being filmed in a studio, as many Westerns were prior to 1930, Walsh's movie was shot on locations across the American West.

prop men and electricians talk about these people who go Hollywood [acquire inflated egos]. And I know that nobody, in Hollywood, can lead a life apart. If you don't act right around the sets, they catch on to you at once, and it doesn't pay.

Wayne enjoyed many aspects of the promotional tour. He especially liked the attention and praise he received from young people when he made appearances at theaters where *The Big Trail* was showing. The droves of autograph seekers greatly flattered him, an attitude he would

19

John Wayne, dressed in a tuxedo, appears at a promotional tour for *The Big Trail*. Although he enjoyed making appearances at theaters for the studio, he detested the studio's practice of inventing a phony biography about him to make his image more romantic and gallant.

retain for the rest of his life. On the other hand, Wayne found some aspects of the tour upsetting. In particular, he disliked the way the studio had invented a phony biography of him designed to make his image more heroic and romantic. According to Fox's press releases, he had been born in the West, had been a Texas Ranger, and was romantically involved with the film's heroine, Marguerite Churchill, in real life as well as on the screen. In truth, Wayne had been born in Iowa, had never even been to Texas much less served as a Ranger, and was not dating his leading lady. He repeatedly frustrated the studio publicity men by telling interviewers the truth about himself.

Unfortunately, despite all of its excellent production values and Fox's vigorous promotion, the film did not do very well at the box office. In general, audiences seemed to agree with the reviews, most of which echoed that of the movie industry publication *Variety.* In October 1930 the paper declared:

> *The Big Trail* will do a certain business because of its magnitude, but it is not a holdover picture. . . . Failing to own a kick or a punch, other than scenically, and with no outstanding cast names, *Trail,* as big as it is and 125 minutes long, remains still a "western" of the American pioneer sort, so thoroughly made familiar by those silent epics preceding it.

The film's mediocre box office showing did more than just disappoint Wayne. As most studios tended to do when a film did not make its money back, Fox reasoned that the public's lack of interest in the picture included its players. So the studio suddenly stopped promoting Wayne's image and otherwise grooming him for stardom. Directors no longer considered him for roles in important films and he became just another of the hundreds of minor players under contract to the studio. His career demotion was reflected in his next film, *Girls Demand Excitement* (1931), a project considered by most to be as cheap and inane as its title, in which he played the captain of a men's basketball team in a coed college. It became increasingly clear that he was not going to become a star overnight as he had thought. It was going to take a long time and a lot of patience and hard work. But Wayne had never been afraid of hard work. More important, he had briefly tasted the thrill and professional satisfaction of stardom and he was willing to do whatever it took to recapture that feeling. For him, there was no going back to being Marion Morrison the prop man. Whatever might come, he was John Wayne, an actor, and he was in it for the long haul.

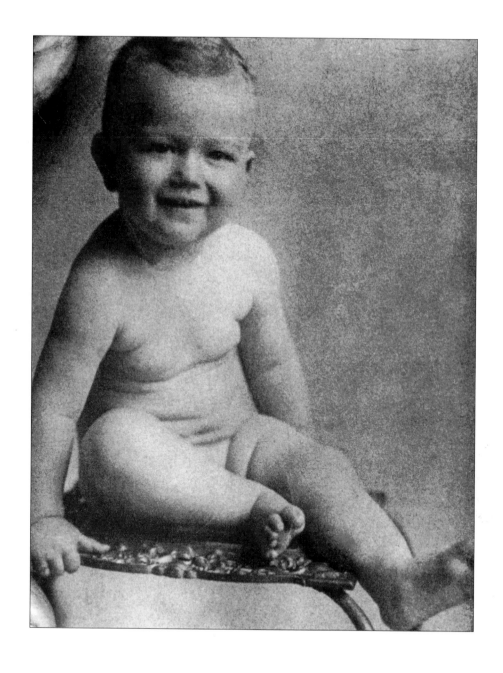

2 The Duke of Glendale

I T WAS PERHAPS FITTING that the man who would come to symbolize the male American hero and old-fashioned American values was a product of what is often referred to as America's heartland. John Wayne was born Marion Robert "Michael" Morrison on May 26, 1907, in the small Iowa town of Winterset, located about 35 miles southwest of Des Moines. The county seat of Madison County, known then as now for its historic covered bridges, Winterset, with a population of less than 4,000, rested in the midst of rich, rolling farm country.

Marion was the first child born to Clyde Morrison, a 23-year-old store clerk, and his 22-year-old wife, Mary, known to family and friends as Molly. Hoping to build a profitable business, in 1910 the elder Morrison moved the family to Earlham, a town even smaller than Winterset, located about 18 miles to the northwest. There, the young couple bought a small drugstore and attempted to put down roots in the community. They had a second son, Robert, the following year and worked hard to make the store a success. However, Clyde and Molly soon began to fight over how the business

---

Marion Robert Morrison was born on May 26, 1907, in Winterset, Iowa. When Marion's brother, Robert, was born in 1911, Marion's middle name became Michael.

should be run. Molly felt that her husband, who tended to extend credit liberally to the customers, was too generous and easygoing and that the store had to be run with a firmer hand.

Marion was too young to understand why his parents fought. He only knew that it made him nervous and afraid and that he wanted to escape the bickering any way he could. At the age of five he frequently hopped aboard freight trains passing through Earlham, and his frantic mother would sometimes find him miles away in another town.

Eventually, the family business was failing badly enough that Clyde thought it best to move the family again. This time, he accepted an offer from his father, who owned 80 acres of land in Lancaster, California, to try his hand at farming. In the summer of 1914, the Morrisons made the move to the West Coast, where Clyde did his best to cultivate corn and beans on the

This four-room white farm cottage on South Second Street in Winterset, Iowa, is the birthplace of Marion Morrison. The house, which today is open to the public, has been restored to its 1907 appearance and contains exhibits about John Wayne's early life and movie career.

arid patch of land on the edge of the barren Mojave Desert. But this new venture turned out no better than the last. According to Shepherd and Slatzer:

> It was a hard life in Lancaster. Clyde worked from sunrise to sundown on the eighty acres, and [Marion] wasn't old enough to be any real help—though he did shuck corn at harvesttime until his hands bled. Their nearest neighbor was at least a mile away, and there was nothing resembling the social life Molly had grown accustomed to in Iowa. As time passed and it seemed that they were making no progress at all, Clyde and Molly began fighting again.

Although he sometimes used the farm's horse to make the six-mile round-trip to school, young Marion often had to walk it. He dreaded going at all because of the way the other children treated him. As Wayne's daughter Aissa recounts in her biography of her father:

> Tall for his age and still exceedingly thin, he also spoke with an accent his California schoolmates had never heard. My father was ridiculed, especially for his name, which he despised. The older boys called Marion "little girl." They asked him why he wore pants instead of a skirt. I think one of the reasons my father frequently acted so macho in later life was to compensate for his childhood torment; I believe it scarred him deeply.

Thanks to such treatment and his parents' renewed fighting, Marion disliked living on the farm and, as he had in Iowa, longed to escape.

The boy soon got his wish. He was nine in June 1916 when, deciding that the farm was a failure, Clyde and Molly moved with the boys to Glendale, California, about five miles from Hollywood, then a quiet village outside of Los Angeles. In Glendale, Marion finally found a measure of the childhood normalcy for which he had been yearning for so long. At the time, the town of 8,000 was growing steadily and jobs were fairly easy to

Sitting on a bench, Marion (left) and Robert Morrison pose for a photograph, circa 1914. In the summer of 1914, the Morrisons moved to Lancaster, California, where Marion often had to make the six-mile trip to and from school on foot.

find. Clyde landed a position at a drugstore and young Marion delivered newspapers and prescriptions in order to earn pocket money. The family was still far from being well-off. For lodging, all Clyde could afford was a run-down rental home, and from the age of 12, Marion had to use his own pocket money to buy school clothes for himself and his brother.

Despite such hardships, however, Marion found plenty to be happy about. He had a number of neighborhood friends, with some of whom he played sandlot baseball and football. With another group, which sported the name the Louise Street Gang, Marion played elaborate games in which the boys imagined themselves to be movie actors portraying cowboys, Indians, and pirates. Sometimes, one boy would pretend to be the director,

while others took the roles of cameramen and actors. The gang members adored movies, which at the time were silent and in black and white, but which held them enraptured for hours on many a Saturday afternoon at the local film house. Marion particularly liked the swashbuckling hero Douglas Fairbanks, Sr., and sometimes leaped from garage roofs to trees, or vice versa, trying to emulate his idol's illustrious stunt theatrics.

Marion also learned about movies firsthand. Because Hollywood was so near his home, he sometimes witnessed film companies shooting scenes on streets or in vacant lots. Occasionally he offered to help the grips, or camera and equipment handlers, and in exchange for lugging lights, props, or other items around the set, he received a box lunch. He was thrilled at the privilege of watching one of the best-known actresses of the day, Pearl White, at work on one of her films. He was also rather shocked when the director aimed some foul language at his leading lady when she failed to complete a shot the way he wanted. "That's the first time I ever heard a man swear at a woman," the grown-up John Wayne later recalled.

Marion had other reasons to be happy. For the first time in his life he enjoyed school, in large part because the other children no longer ribbed him about his name. Instead of Marion, they called him by what he considered the manly nickname Duke. According to Alan Barbour:

As the story is often told, he owned a large Airedale dog named "Duke." When he went to school he would leave the animal in the care of some friendly firemen at the local firehouse. The men nicknamed the dog's master "Little Duke" and the "Little" was dropped as [Marion] grew tall. "Duke" persisted over the years.

Almost as if the new name had given him a fresh identity, Duke Morrison excelled at school and impressed his

Daredevil actor Douglas Fairbanks, Sr., appears here in costume in an undated photograph. Marion enjoyed going to the swashbuckler's films, which include *The Mark of Zorro, The Thief of Bagdad,* and *The Black Pirate.*

teachers. One of his eighth-grade instructors, Vera Brinn, later recalled, "I used to tell the students to choose their own seats. New students always take seats way back. Not [Duke]. He sat down in the front row of seats, close to my desk." According to Brinn and other teachers, Duke was an intelligent, attentive student who always seemed to know the answers when called upon.

The young man continued to excel when he entered Glendale High School in 1921. He maintained a B average, joined the Latin club, and became prop man for the school's drama productions. He also became vice-president of his junior class and first-semester president of his senior class. In addition, he played football, wrote sports articles for the school newspaper, and represented the school at a Shakespeare recital contest attended by students from all around Southern California.

Yet Duke was not quite the complete model student. He had a sly sense of humor and enjoyed playing practical jokes, a pastime he would later periodically enjoy as an adult on Hollywood movie sets. Sometimes one of his high school pranks got him into trouble. In perhaps the most memorable incident, he and a friend smuggled bottles into school, each containing a chemical so foul-smelling that it caused nausea. They sprinkled the noxious liquid around the halls and classrooms and the stench was so bad that the school had to be closed for the day. Eventually the boys got caught and had to apologize in front of an assembly of all the students and teachers.

Duke also picked up another bad habit when he was in high school, one he retained for nearly the rest of his life—the liberal use of alcohol. His first experience with being intoxicated was at age 16. He remembered later,

> After that [first drunk], I would drink almost every week-
> end, and I didn't like dating girls who were against my

drinking. . . . [I ran with] probably the toughest roughest gang of guys in the Glendale High School. . . . I didn't usually hang around with them except for drinking and drag racing and picking up a certain type of girl on Saturday nights. I just kept my drinking companions separated from my refined Glendale friends.

Duke also managed to keep his drinking and other questionable after-school activities separate from his academics and sports endeavors. He continued to maintain good grades in his senior year and helped lead the school football team to the Southern California high school championship in 1925. His performances on the gridiron seemed so promising, in fact, that he received an offer for a scholarship to nearby USC. The six-foot-four-inch-tall young man wanted to attend college and realized that without the scholarship he would not be able to afford to go, so he gratefully accepted.

Duke Morrison entered USC in September 1925 as a pre-law student. Because his family could not assist him financially, the school arranged for him to earn spending money by working part-time at the local telephone company and by waiting tables and washing dishes at the Sigma Chi fraternity house. As part of the deal, Duke received room and board as a member of the fraternity. After a while he also made extra money by appearing, along with some of his football buddies, in movies, although at the time he had no intention of pursuing acting as a career. His friend and teammate, Pexy Eckles, later said:

Movies with college themes or backgrounds, particularly collegiate football, were very popular at the time. Nearly all the studios were making them, and so were coming over to USC and using students as extras. Duke worked as a football player in several of them, along with other members of the team. . . . I remember that one of them was filmed in the Rose Bowl; I don't recall any of their titles,

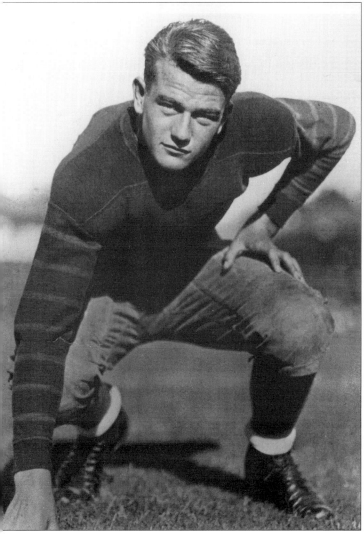

Freshman Duke Morrison of the University of Southern California (USC) is seen here as a member of the USC football team in 1925. Without the football scholarship that USC awarded him, Morrison would not have been able to afford college.

though; they weren't important films, and there were quite a few of them. . . . Duke and I enjoyed such work and were grateful for the pay, which was about eight or ten dollars a day—good money back then.

While attending USC, Duke met Josephine "Josie" Saenz, a young Los Angeles woman whose Spanish father was a Panamanian diplomat assigned to the United

States. She was petite, with a shapely figure, flowing black hair, and large, unusually expressive eyes. Their first date affected him deeply, for he knew immediately that she was different from any of the women he had ever known. And at seeing, hearing, and touching her, a new and very pleasant feeling seemed to wash over him. Duke Morrison suspected that he was falling in love. Many years later he remembered standing with Josie on that first date at the beach and watching the waves roll in:

> I was full of feelings I never had felt before. I was so hypnotized I don't think I said more than two words that night. I remember opening the door of the car for her, and my fingers happened to graze her arm. . . . A shiver went through me. I knew I must be in love. I had read about it in stories, seen love scenes in the movies, read love poems about feelings like this, so I knew this was what it had to be. . . . They never tell you how much it hurts. They don't tell you it hurts from the start and I guess it never stops hurting, but it sure is a beautiful feeling to have.

Not long after Duke and Josie began dating, the young man experienced the first of a series of abrupt, and at the time painful, changes in his family and school life. In May 1926, his mother filed for divorce from his father. She got custody of 15-year-old Robert and moved to the nearby town of Long Beach, while Clyde moved into an apartment in Los Angeles. This meant that Duke no longer had a home to go back to in the summer or during holidays. Luckily, he managed to arrange a deal with his fraternity house and spent the summer of 1926 there.

A few months later, another blow struck. The school informed Duke that his scholarship would not be renewed. Although he was a competent football player and worked as hard as he could on the field, he was not in the same league as many of the all-American-caliber players on the USC team and his coaches could not justify the expense of his scholarship. He had to leave the frat house and, somewhat despondent and embarrassed, accepted a generous invitation from his friend Pexy Eckles and his family to live above their garage. Duke hoped to give football another try in the fall of 1927, perhaps to make a last-ditch effort to get his scholarship back. But because of a shoulder injury, this time he was unable even to make the team. He had no money to continue his education or, for that matter, to pay Pexy's parents for the garage room. Duke's only alternative was to find a full-time job.

In May 1926, Duke's mother, photographed here many years later with her actor son, divorced her husband and moved to Long Beach, California, with her son Robert. Meanwhile Duke had to endure the distressing change in his family life and make arrangements to spend the summer at his fraternity house at USC.

Fortunately, finding work turned out to be easy. Duke had worked part-time as a laborer on the Fox movie lot during his summers at USC, a job that had been arranged by the school's athletic department. His bosses on the lot liked him and considered him hardworking and trustworthy, so they happily found him a full-time position. In November 1927, Duke became an assistant prop man for $35 per week. Often putting in 14-hour days, he regularly transported furniture, books, and hundreds of smaller props from one movie set to another and helped the senior prop men dress the sets.

But though he liked prop work, or propping, and decided to make a career of it, Duke was not content with a salary of $35 per week. It was plenty for him to live on as a young single man, but he wanted to marry Josie and support her in style, and to that end he planned to save up as much money as he could. So he frequently made extra cash by playing bit parts in some of the Fox studio's films during temporary lulls in his propping duties. His first screen appearance since the football films he had done while at USC was in 1928 in *Hangman's House*. According to Aissa Wayne,

> [It was] the first time John Wayne's face could clearly be seen on celluloid [film]. He played an Irish peasant, a spectator at a horse race, who takes off his white cap at the end of a thrilling finish, busts down a white picket fence with some other fans, and sprints into the track. It was a turning point in his life. Seeing himself on screen . . . gave new rise to his dreams.

Duke's first screen credit, his only one as Duke Morrison, came in 1929 in *Words and Music,* a musical that took place at a college and in which he had a small and forgettable role as a student. Shortly after working on this film, Duke had his unexpected and incredibly fortunate encounter on the lot with the director Raoul Walsh, who subsequently cast him in the multimillion-dollar production *The Big Trail.* After that, his screen credits always carried the name that Walsh and studio boss Winfield Sheehan had chosen for him—John Wayne.

But at the time, the name John Wayne did not carry the same weight, onscreen or offscreen, that it would later. Despite his first major role, the young actor was far from being a household name. Thanks to *The Big Trail*'s disappointing box office showing and the studio's decision not to groom him for stardom, Wayne faced an uphill battle. He realized that in order to become successful he would have to take whatever roles he could get, work hard at learning the acting trade, and hope to get another break as big as the one Walsh had given him. But whatever happened, he reasoned, the important thing was that he was lucky enough to be doing something he found fascinating and personally rewarding. As Aissa Wayne put it: "For better and worse, John Wayne was hooked on making movies."

3 King of the Pecos

FOR JOHN WAYNE, the 1930s was the period during which he learned his craft. He worked steadily and hard for a number of different studios and made dozens of B movies, films turned out quickly, on shoestring budgets, and generally of second-rate quality. These Bs were mostly Westerns with words such as *range, sagebrush, trail, Pecos,* and other references to the Wild West in their titles. Invariably, Wayne was typecast as the good guy who walked tall, talked tough, vanquished the villains, and got the girl at the end of the picture. He played so many Western heroes, in fact, that it became difficult for producers and directors in the film business to envision him playing anything else and he rarely received offers to do non-Westerns.

Although he made a lot of films, he was a long way from being considered a real movie star. That enviable status was reserved for a few dozen nationally and internationally popular actors and actresses, people such as Gary Cooper, Bette Davis, Spencer Tracy, and Joan Crawford. They were stars partly because they had a certain hard-to-define quality, a widespread appeal that made them household names around the world. They were also "bankable,"

In *The Big Stampede* Wayne's character confronts an evil cattle baron, played by Noah Beery. Wayne made the B Western for Warner Bros. in 1932, the year he was also making serials for Mascot.

meaning that any producer who cast them in a film could usually count on their drawing power at the box office to make the film a financial success.

By contrast, as a B actor John Wayne was far from being a household name. As a rule, B movies were considered filler to round out double bills at theaters and were not heavily promoted or advertised. Many of these films played only in certain parts of the country and the majority were not seen in other countries, so any one B movie or B player had a limited audience. Because of these factors, Wayne's name had little or no drawing power,

In the 1930s Wayne was continually typecast as the "good guy" who walked tall, talked tough, and vanquished the villains— in this scene from *The Big Stampede* he is even outnumbered three to one.

so he was not bankable. Certainly, part of his B status in this early stage of his career was a result of his lack of acting experience and technique. As biographer Alan Barbour points out:

> Looking objectively at these early films, one must conclude that Wayne simply wasn't ready for stardom. He had a lot to learn about screen technique. His movements were awkward, his speech unmodulated and unconvincing. . . . He did, however, possess good looks, abundant athletic ability and an apparently limitless amount of energy, combined with the willingness to work hard and learn. The effort paid off well in the long run, for when stardom did beckon he was ready and able to meet the challenge. There's an actor's expression which sums up Wayne's labors rather neatly: "He paid his dues."

At first, Wayne paid his dues in Fox studio B films such as *Girls Demand Excitement* and *Three Girls Lost.* He realized that the quality of these films was far below that of *The Big Trail.* But by the end of 1930, he was making $200 per week, almost three times what he had made on *Trail,* and he took some consolation in the fact that he was at least earning a decent living. He still wanted to someday marry Josie, whom he continued to date regularly, and he was happy to be making enough to save for the future. This comfortable feeling evaporated rather abruptly, however, when Fox canceled his contract early in 1931. Apparently, the studio felt he had no future in the movies.

Wayne now faced making an important decision. He could return to propping, in effect a giant step backward, or he could approach other studios and continue his quest for acting success. For Wayne—young, eager, and energetic—the second choice was the only logical one, and he met with Harry Cohn, head of Columbia Pictures. Cohn signed Wayne to a five-year contract at $300 a week and cast him as the romantic lead—the role of a

West Point graduate pursuing his girlfriend to a remote western army post—in *Arizona*. It seemed to Wayne that his Columbia deal represented a promising new start for his career.

But once more he was disappointed. Wayne soon found himself the unenviable object of Harry Cohn's infamous wrath. The studio boss got the mistaken idea that Wayne had been romantically involved with an actress in the cast of *Arizona*, a young woman Cohn himself was seeing. Cohn got his revenge in 1931 by casting Wayne in a series of lackluster supporting roles in B movies. For example, in Columbia's *Range Feud*, Wayne played a young rancher falsely accused of murder, and in *Maker of Men*, a football picture, his role as a gridiron player was barely more than a bit part. Other small roles followed, including that of a corpse in *The Deceiver*. At this point, Wayne was so fed up that he was not sorry when Cohn got his final revenge by canceling his contract.

Refusing to be defeated by this new setback, Wayne set out again to make the rounds of the studios. This time, however, he took the advice of his actor friend, Paul Fix, who suggested that finding work might be a great deal easier if Wayne had an agent to represent him. In 1931, Wayne signed on with the Leo Morrison Agency, which handled well-known stars such as Spencer Tracy and Jean Harlow, as well as many lesser-known performers. The agent assigned to represent Wayne, Al Kingston, immediately took a liking to the handsome young actor. According to Shepherd and Slatzer:

> Kingston had seen Duke in *The Big Trail* and had liked his performance. And after talking to him for a while, he liked Duke personally, too. What particularly impressed him was Duke's genuine modesty and honesty and the fact that he didn't expect Kingston to work miracles on his behalf.

He neither asked nor expected the agency to get him starring roles. Duke told him that he would take any acting job Kingston could get him and that he'd work hard to prove himself worthy of Kingston's efforts.

Kingston introduced Wayne to Nat Levine, who became known in the business as the "king of the serials." Serials were long, usually low-budget action-adventure films that theaters showed in a series of short segments, or chapters, each chapter preceding the A and B films on a typical double bill. Levine's Mascot Pictures turned out many serials, as well as regular feature films, most of them B movies. Like Kingston, Levine had liked John Wayne in *The Big Trail* and also found the young actor's personality engaging. Levine later remembered:

> I was impressed with his honesty, his character. You could *believe* him. There was nothing phony about the guy, and that came through on the screen. As an actor, he wasn't the best and he wasn't the worst. He was okay. What helped him more than anything else was his naturalness—along the lines of Spencer Tracy.

Late in 1931, Levine offered Wayne a contract that promised to pay him $100 per week for the first year, $150 per week for the second, and $200 per week for the third. Although this was less than Wayne had been making previously, Levine sweetened the deal by making the contract nonexclusive. This meant that the actor only had to work for Mascot for six months of the year, during the remainder of which he could make films for other studios and producers and continue to draw his Mascot salary. Wayne's first picture for Mascot was a serial called *Shadow of the Eagle,* in which he portrayed a stunt pilot who traveled with a circus. The film was notable only in that it was during its shooting that Wayne met Yakima Canutt, a former rodeo champion who was regarded as one of the best stunt coordinators working in movies. It

John Wayne and Josie Saenz held their wedding at the Los Angeles home of their friend, actress Loretta Young, on June 24, 1933.

was the beginning of a lifelong professional and personal relationship.

In 1932, Wayne did other serials for Mascot, including *The Hurricane Express,* in which he again played a pilot, this time on the trail of an archvillain known as the

Wrecker. While working for Levine, Wayne took full advantage of his nonexclusive contract and acted in pictures for other studios. Among these were *Lady and Gent* for Paramount Pictures and a series of B Westerns for Warner Bros. Pictures, including *Haunted Gold, Ride Him Cowboy,* and *The Big Stampede.* Because he had constant work and often drew two paychecks, Wayne felt at last in a financial position to marry Josie, and they had a small but formal ceremony at a friend's home on June 24, 1933.

Wayne and his new bride had no time for a honeymoon because shortly before the wedding he had signed a contract to do eight B Westerns for Monogram Pictures, a small studio run by film executive Trem Carr. These films, known as the Lone Star Pictures, were scheduled to begin shooting immediately, so the young couple had just enough time to move into their comfortable new apartment before Wayne returned to work. He made it up to Josie in the next two years, however. Between his Mascot and Monogram contracts, he averaged more than $700 per week in 1933 and 1934, at the height of the Great Depression when millions of people were out of work and the average salary of those who did have jobs was between $20 and $25 per week. Making such good money allowed Wayne, in his occasional off-work hours, to take Josie to expensive restaurants, nightspots, and sporting events.

The deal with Monogram turned out to be lucrative for Wayne because he ended up making 16 Lone Star Westerns rather than 8. Although important film critics generally ignored them, as they did most B pictures, these Westerns, with colorful titles such as *Riders of Destiny, The Lawless Frontier, The Star Packer,* and *Texas Terror,* proved popular in midwestern and western states and turned a profit. Each ran about 55 minutes, had a budget of about $15,000, and took 10 to 15 days to shoot.

Because all of these films were shot on locations near the studio, in the then sparsely populated San Fernando and Simi valleys, they had the same visual look of most Westerns turned out by other studios, which utilized the same locations.

But the Lone Star Pictures were faster paced and more realistic than most competing B Westerns. The lion's share of credit for this went to Yakima Canutt, who played many of the Lone Star villains and designed the many complicated and dangerous stunts, and also to Wayne, who helped his friend stage the exciting fight scenes. Before the two men teamed up in the Lone Star films, Shepherd and Slatzer explained in their book about Wayne,

barroom brawls and fistfights in Westerns were ridiculous. The stuntmen wrestled, mostly, and in order to avoid serious injury to one another, whatever punches they threw

In January 1934, Wayne and his wife, Josie, sun-bathe with movie luminary Spencer Tracy (wearing sunglasses) at a desert resort in Palm Springs, California. Despite the Great Depression, Wayne made good money, which enabled him to take his wife to fashionable resorts, restaurants, and nightclubs.

were aimed at arms and shoulders, resulting in what looked about as menacing as a schoolyard fight between two youngsters whose hearts weren't in the battle. Duke and Yak addressed the problem by choreographing their fights and developing what they called the Pass System, whereby one of them would aim with full force at the other's chin and narrowly miss it, while the other went crashing through breakaway tables and the like from the apparent blow. . . . Robert Bradbury [the director] . . . began cutting the action and placing the camera behind the person throwing the punch, so that it was impossible to see that the blows weren't landing.

The sound effects of the blows were added later. The Canutt-Wayne Pass System, which quickly became the film industry standard for staging realistic fight scenes, is still widely used today.

Although Wayne was generally satisfied with his work for Monogram, one aspect of these productions bothered him. In the first Lone Star Picture, *Riders of Destiny,* he was cast as Singin' Sandy Saunders, in the studio's attempt to cash in on the popularity of singing cowboys, such as Western star Gene Autry. Wayne thought that guitar-toting cowboys were effeminate, or unmanly, and, perhaps remembering his childhood problems with his feminine-sounding name, he did not want to mar his image as a macho cowboy hero. So he soon managed to persuade his bosses not to keep Singin' Sandy as a recurring character. As Aissa Wayne explains:

> In truth, my father could not sing at all, nor play the guitar. So while Hollywood dubbed it—two men would stand off-camera, one singing, one strumming—my father faked it. . . . In those days, my father said, Hollywood cowboys were "pretty," with their snow-white Stetsons [hats], their uncreased faces, their tender . . . voices. . . . Once he begged out of this "embarrassing" role, my father said he shattered the mold forever, evolving the Hollywood cowboy into a steely, masculine loner.

45

John Wayne was finishing the last of the Lone Star Pictures early in 1935 when a large studio merger occurred that would have a major impact on his career. Herbert Yates, the head of Consolidated Film Industries, a company that specialized in processing film for various production companies and producers, masterminded a deal that combined his company with both the Mascot and Monogram studios. The resulting new and larger company was known as Republic Pictures. Planning to continue Monogram's successful run of B Westerns, Republic immediately signed Wayne to do another eight cowboy epics. The studio also signed Canutt and many other actors and technicians who had worked on the Lone Star films. The production pace for the new Western series was frantic, and in only about a year Wayne completed all eight films, among them *Westward Ho, The Lawless Range, King of the Pecos,* and *The Lonely Trail.*

In June 1936, with *Winds of the Wasteland,* the last of the eight Republic Westerns, "in the can," or finished, the studio offered Wayne a long-term contract with a salary of $24,000 per year. The actor was tempted to accept, but Trem Carr, who had recently left Republic and joined Universal Pictures, made him an even better offer—to play lead roles in six B films and receive $6,000 for each. Because the six projects would take about a year to complete, Wayne would make $36,000. Partly for financial reasons, Wayne decided to go with the Universal deal. He and Josie now had two young children—Michael, born in November 1934, and Toni, born in February 1936—and he felt that ensuring the family's future financial security should be his main priority. Among the roles he played for the Universal series were a U.S. Coast Guard commander in *The Sea Spoilers,* a newsreel cameraman in *I Cover the War,* and a hockey player in *Idol of the Crowds.*

In the spring of 1937, while finishing the last of the Universal films, Wayne took a long and sober look at his career situation. He had worked hard and almost relentlessly for years and his acting had become increasingly competent and polished. He felt that he was as good as Gary Cooper and many other top stars who made far more money than he did and that it was about time for his hard work to pay off with a break into stardom. But such breaks were rare, Wayne knew, and he began to worry that he might remain the king of the B pictures for the rest of his life.

Wayne had no way of knowing that the big break he longed for was already in its planning stages. His first inkling came early in the summer of 1937 when the well-known director John Ford invited him for a cruise on Ford's boat. Wayne had known Ford for years, having

Wayne punches an enemy in Paramount's *Shepherd of the Hills*, released in 1941 and based on a story by novelist Harold Bell Wright. The picture, which portrays the conflict between strangers who try to buy land in the Ozark mountains and the Ozarkers who try to combat the outsiders, makes use of the Canutt-Wayne Pass System, the method of staging realistic fight scenes.

47

The Waynes became parents for the first time with the birth of their son Michael Anthony in November 1934. After the birth of his daughter Toni two years later, Wayne decided to opt for a contract with Universal, in which he could make $36,000 in one year.

worked as a prop man and bit player in the late 1920s on a few of the director's early films, including *Hangman's House*. Ford showed Wayne a story, titled "Stage to Lordsburg," that had appeared in a recent issue of *Collier's* magazine. Without mentioning that he wanted to make a film version of the story with Wayne as the lead, Ford asked his friend to read it and offer a critique.

"It's a fine story," said Wayne.

"Who do you think would be good as the Ringo Kid?" Ford asked.

"Lloyd Nolan."

"Nolan!" Ford thundered. "Duke, you dumb son-ofabitch! Don't you think *you* could handle the part?"

"Well, hell yes, Coach," Wayne answered. "If I had the opportunity."

"You'll have the opportunity," the director promised.

True to his word, Ford cast Wayne as the Ringo Kid in a Western titled *Stagecoach*. This was to be a very different kind of Western than Wayne had been used to. Ford was a major director and the film would receive first-class billing, widespread promotion and theatrical release, and attention by important film critics. As he awaited word on when shooting would begin, the realization that his hard work had paid off filled Wayne with both joy and nervous anticipation. He had made the A list at last. Nearly a decade later than he had originally expected, he was finally going to be a real movie star.

Reaping the Wild Wind of Fame

4

WHEN IT WAS RELEASED IN 1939, the film *Stagecoach* made John Wayne a star, and he never had to make another B movie for the rest of his long career. Suddenly bankable and successful, he now enjoyed the luxury of choosing from the best scripts, as well as the material rewards of fame. His salary per picture soared, giving him the money to do whatever he wanted whenever he wanted, and people from all walks of life and from nearly every corner of the globe accorded him instant recognition and respect. Yet at the same time that his career took off, his private life began to have some decided ups and downs. He seemed unable simultaneously to maintain a successful movie career and a happy home life and established a pattern of remarriage and divorce that brought him both personal pain and negative publicity.

Wayne's private problems developed gradually, however, and were not yet apparent in November 1938 when shooting began on *Stagecoach*. His marriage to Josie still relatively stable at the time, the 31-year-old actor concen-

Dallas (Claire Trevor) and the Ringo Kid (Wayne) exchange a yearning glance as they make coffee in a scene from John Ford's classic Western *Stagecoach*. The great epic of 1939 made John Wayne a star.

trated all of his energies on the film project that promised to completely reshape his career. Wayne realized that the film's script, adapted by Dudley Nichols from the *Collier's* story, was not particularly original or innovative. The script depicts a group of diverse individuals thrown together by fate in a stagecoach journey. Along the way, they meet a wanted man—the Ringo Kid, the role in which John Ford had cast Wayne—who is headed for a showdown with a gang of outlaws. During a series of adventures, including a spectacular escape from attacking Indians across some dried salt flats and the final showdown with the outlaws, the Ringo Kid falls for one of the passengers, a saloon dancer, and they ride away together into the sunset.

Wayne was thoroughly confident, though, that Ford's choice of actors and skill as a director, as well as the high production values afforded by a decent budget, would more than make up for the story's lack of originality. And this was indeed the case. Ford assembled a distinguished cast, including veteran character actors Thomas Mitchell, John Carradine, and George Bancroft, along with the popular star Claire Trevor. The director also hired top cinematographer Bert Glennon and legendary stunt coordinator and Wayne's old friend Yakima Canutt and scheduled shooting at more than a dozen scenic locations in California and Arizona. When it came to delivering screen quality, Ford meant business, a fact Wayne learned the hard way on the *Stagecoach* set. As Alan Barbour tells it:

> Ford did not give Wayne an easy time during the filming. He berated, cajoled, tormented, tricked and otherwise abused the insecure actor into giving the best performance of his career to that date. At the time Ford may have seemed insensitive to the feelings of the younger man, but the director realized that he would have to be brutal to raise the level of Wayne's performance to that of the other

players. He was determined to keep Wayne from doing a weak and ineffectual job in contrast to the polished acting of the professionals surrounding him. It worked, and one need only view Wayne's performances in films released the same year to see the remarkable difference.

Although Ford's sometimes harsh treatment of him during shooting irritated Wayne, the actor quickly put any negative feelings for the director behind him. Wayne saw that Ford's uncompromising demands for quality from his actors and technicians paid off handsomely in the long run. *Stagecoach* became a huge box office success and also received rave reviews. Thomas Mitchell received the 1939 Oscar for best supporting actor in the film and Ford garnered the New York Critics' Award for best director. Although Wayne's own critical notices for his role as the Ringo Kid were generally good, they were not raves. Nevertheless, the fact that he had held his own in a cast of seasoned professionals in a widely acclaimed A-level movie made him both bankable and in demand. Offers began to stream in from producers and studios who, before *Stagecoach*'s release, would not have given him an interview.

Wayne realized that he needed sound professional advice to help him choose from the many offers he was receiving and to guide his newfound stardom. His contract with the Leo Morrison Agency had run out early in 1939 and he promptly signed on with Charles K. Feldman, one of the best and most influential agents in the business. Feldman renegotiated Wayne's contract with Republic Pictures. Under the terms of the five-year deal, the actor agreed to star in at least two movies annually for the studio, which promised to work its schedule around any other projects he might be doing for other studios. Feldman also fielded Wayne's film offers, suggested which would best promote his image and career, and negotiated large salaries for his client. The first two pictures Wayne did under the guidance of his new agent were *Allegheny Uprising,* a big-budget frontier epic, and *The Dark Command,* a Republic Western directed by Raoul Walsh, who had discovered Wayne a decade earlier.

Not long after completing *The Dark Command,* Wayne went to work on another John Ford film—*The Long Voyage Home.* His role in the film, that of a Swedish sailor named Ole Olsen, proved to be one of the most unusual of his career and one that he always looked back on with a great deal of personal satisfaction. According to Alan Barbour:

> Because we are so used to Wayne's stylized manner of speech, it is a little difficult for today's filmgoers to accept his broad Swedish accent, but on the film's initial release in 1940 it was considered very successful. The story was based on a series of one-act plays by [the renowned playwright] Eugene O'Neill. . . . A group of men . . . sail aboard the *Glencairn* for London with a cargo of high explosives. On the long journey hostility among the men erupts into violence, until the ship is attacked by enemy planes. . . . O'Neill was quoted as saying that he enjoyed this film version of his work more than any other adapted from his plays. It also marked Wayne's last attempt to use an accent that wasn't his own.

When *The Long Voyage Home* received enthusiastic critical reviews and made a tidy profit for United Artists, the studio that had released it, Wayne's career seemed to move into high gear. In rapid succession, he made *Three Faces West* and *Lady from Louisiana* for Republic and *Seven Sinners* for Universal. Then Cecil B. DeMille, the director known for his spectacular epics, such as *The Ten Commandments* (1923) and *Cleopatra* (1934), asked Wayne to star in *Reap the Wild Wind,* an adventure story about a ship captain accused of murder. Wayne's first color film, it featured romance, intrigue, and a dramatic fight to the death with a giant squid on the ocean bottom. DeMille was one of the biggest names in Hollywood at the time and the public eagerly awaited his films. Starring in a DeMille picture was a symbol of having "made it" in the film industry and Wayne looked forward to a long and prosperous career.

Soon after *Reap the Wild Wind*'s successful opening in 1942, however, the United States entered World War II and Wayne suddenly found himself wondering about his future. Should he enlist in the service and interrupt his career, perhaps permanently, or continue making

In Cecil B. DeMille's adventure *Reap the Wild Wind,* Wayne plays a sea captain who must fend off a giant squid. The 1942 picture was Wayne's first color film, and acting for DeMille meant that Wayne had finally made it in the movie business.

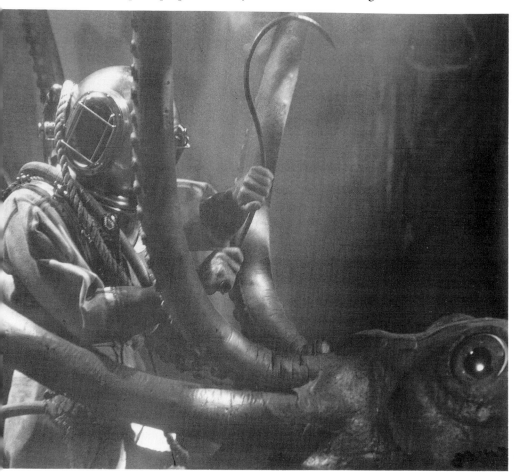

films and ensure the professional momentum he had already built up? He certainly had no obligation to enlist. As a 34-year-old with 4 children—his son Patrick and daughter Melinda having been born in 1939 and 1940 respectively—he was exempt from the military draft. Yet other older Hollywood figures were enlisting, including his friend John Ford, who was in his forties at the time.

Wayne eventually chose not to enlist. Of course, he and his agent recognized the importance of providing an explanation for the public, which might see a contradiction between Wayne's not serving and his popular macho screen image. As Shepherd and Slatzer put it:

> Although it was rumored that Duke had tried to enlist but had been turned down because of a broken eardrum and an old shoulder injury, the evidence indicates that he simply exercised his right by law to stay out of the service. Those who later saw John Wayne as the embodiment of superpatriotism couldn't conceive of his *choosing* not to enlist, and so "excuses" were fashioned to conform to their image of him. This was just another example of the kind of claim that Duke publicly ignored but privately discounted by saying, "Hell, *I* didn't say that about me. *They* said that about me!"

Even though he did not serve his country in uniform, Wayne did his part to help with the war effort. He made a number of appearances with the United Service Organizations (USO), which brought entertainment of all types to the troops, both at home and in camps overseas. In addition to participating in a 90-day USO–sponsored trip to New Guinea in the South Pacific, Wayne frequently visited wounded servicemen in U.S. hospitals.

Wayne also contributed indirectly to the war effort by making a number of patriotic war films designed not only to make money but also to boost the morale of the American people. In his first war film, *Flying Tigers,* released in 1942, he played a fighter pilot commander.

Reunion in France, in which he again portrayed a fighter pilot, this time one who crashes in Nazi-occupied France, immediately followed. Among Wayne's other war films were *The Fighting Seabees,* released in 1944, about the brave men who constructed air fields on battle-strewn South Pacific islands, and *Back to Bataan,* released in 1945, the story of the heroic American-Philippine resistance to Japanese aggression.

The cinematic figure of John Wayne as a war hero seemed to strike a new, positive, and highly emotional

John Agar (left), John Wayne, and Forrest Tucker, as U.S. Marines, storm the beach in *Sands of Iwo Jima.* Wayne's portrayal of Sergeant John M. Stryker as a realistic, vulnerable leader earned Wayne an Oscar nomination.

Wayne plays with sons Michael and Patrick in 1942. Wayne's relationship with Josie had become strained during the actor's relentless work schedule, and the two divorced in December 1945.

chord with audiences. Perhaps because his manly image symbolized the toughness and valor most Americans wanted their troops to display, the moviegoing public reacted even more enthusiastically to Wayne in roles as brave GIs than to his portrayals of more standard fictional cowboy and action heroes. In the years immediately

following the war's conclusion, a period in which Hollywood turned out a great many movies with World War II themes, audiences continued to identify strongly with Wayne's soldier image. Perhaps the most popular example was *Sands of Iwo Jima,* released in 1949, in which his character took part in the bloody marine assault on that Japanese-held island, and for which he won his first Academy Award nomination. According to Aissa Wayne:

> His role in *Sands of Iwo Jima,* as Marine Sergeant John M. Stryker, won him more than an Oscar nomination; it had stunning impact on people who saw it. When my father charged up Iwo Jima Hill, only to be cut down by sniper fire just steps from the top, people wept in their seats. Their tears did not go unnoticed by the czars [studio heads] ruling Hollywood. . . . The power brokers came to view my dad as a rare and critical asset. "There's nothing wrong with Hollywood," a producer told *Cosmopolitan* [magazine], "that a dozen John Waynes couldn't cure."

Wayne's macho, patriotic image and his relentless hard work as an actor could not, however, cure his ailing marriage to Josie. Although the two had been happy in the 1930s, their relationship became increasingly strained in the years following his work on *Stagecoach* and sudden attainment of stardom. Josie had never liked the idea that her husband was a workaholic. She had managed to put up with his 14-hour-per-day, often 7-day-per-week, shooting schedules for years, hoping all the while that when he finally became a star he would allow himself the luxuries of slowing down, making fewer films, and spending more time at home. But stardom did not slow Wayne down. As he continued, year after year, to maintain his busy professional commitments, Josie spent most of her time alone and, almost inevitably, the two steadily grew apart. The courts granted Josie a legal separation in 1943 and she and Wayne were legally divorced in December 1945.

Only two weeks after the divorce, on January 17, 1946, Wayne married an aspiring young Mexican actress named Esperanza "Chata" Morrison (who had married a man named Eugene Morrison before she met Wayne) whom he had met on a business trip to Mexico City three years earlier. Many of Wayne's actor friends were surprised that he had married Chata. She had a reputation for loving and leaving dozens of rich actors and playboys, as well as for having a fiery temper. Ward Bond, a well-known character actor whom Wayne had known since his college days at USC, tried to talk him out of tying the knot with Chata. But Wayne would not listen. He felt that he was in love and he strongly believed that the marriage institution was the natural and sacred expression of love between a man and woman.

Shortly after their marriage, Wayne learned the hard way about Chata's temper, which, according to the accounts of family and friends, more than matched his own. During most of their eight years together they fought regularly. Chata also brought her mother from Mexico to live with them. The older woman's habit of getting drunk and falsely accusing him of having affairs with the actresses he kissed onscreen became a constant source of irritation to Wayne. The marriage deteriorated, and he and Chata were divorced in October 1953.

Wayne's seeming attraction to Latin women did not end with his official break with Chata. In November 1954, he married Pilar Palette Weldy, the daughter of a Peruvian senator. Wayne and Pilar's first daughter, Aissa Wayne, born in 1956, later recounted her parents' initial meeting:

> In 1952, his marriage to Chata without hope and the lawyers preparing for court, my father flew to South America [to scout locations for a movie]. . . . When he arrived in Peru, [he] was told to look up Richard Weldy, who worked for Pan-American Grace Airways when he wasn't

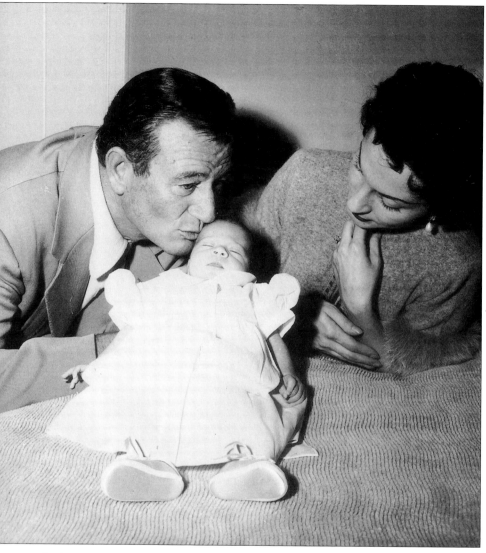

leading tours up the waters of the Amazon. . . . Weldy took my dad to the small jungle town of Tango Maria, where a Peruvian film crew was squarely in the midst of shooting a scene. By the time of their arrival the afternoon sun was dying. By firelight, a young Latin actress [who was married to Weldy at the time] danced barefoot for the camera, her long hair dark and unruly, her legs thin and sculpted. This

In April 1956, Wayne kisses his daughter Aissa as his third wife, Pilar, looks on. Wayne hoped his third marriage would provide the permanent relationship he was seeking.

was the vision that charmed my father the first time he saw my mother.

Wayne hoped that when it came to marriage the number three would prove to be magical, that his union with Pilar would be the permanent relationship he had always longed for but that he seemed to find so elusive. Their first few years together gave him every reason to be hopeful in this regard. Pilar often traveled with him to shooting locations, where they shared many happy moments. And the marriage produced two more children—John, born in 1962, and Marisa, born in 1966.

For Wayne, a man obsessed with making movies, constant work provided an escape from marital problems. In contrast to the squabbles with Josie and Chata that made his private life so stormy and unstable in the 1940s and early 1950s, his career experiences during this same period brought him extraordinary financial rewards, as well as a healthy measure of personal satisfaction and pride. When his Republic contract lapsed early in 1946, Charles Feldman negotiated a special nonexclusive deal for him. The studio agreed to pay the actor a minimum of $150,000 per picture plus a percentage of the gross, or total money taken in at the box office. This allowed Wayne to make more than $200,000 per film, a huge amount at the time. In addition, Wayne had the option to produce any of his own films if he so desired, which not only increased his moneymaking potential but also allowed him to hire and fire people and thereby attain a great deal of power and influence in Hollywood.

Wayne's power in the film industry expanded even further shortly after the 1948 release of the widely popular Western *Red River,* for which he received excellent reviews. Because of his success in that film and those that immediately followed, he made the *Motion Picture Herald'* s top 10 box office star list, a coveted position he would enjoy for more than 23 years. The year 1948 marked another important career milestone for Wayne. Since working with John Ford on *The Long Voyage Home* eight years before, he had done only one Ford film—the war epic *They Were Expendable,* released in 1945. Now, Wayne received an offer to star in a new big-budget Western the director was planning. Unbeknownst to Wayne, he and his old friend were about to form a unique actor-director partnership, a legendary union from which would spring some of the greatest Westerns of all time.

5 A New Monument in the Valley

THE SCREEN COLLABORATION between John Wayne and John Ford in the late 1940s and early 1950s was one of the most successful in Hollywood history. With Ford in the director's chair and Wayne riding tall in the star's saddle, the two men spearheaded a highly creative team of professionals who, in an eight-year period, turned out five superior Western films—*Fort Apache, Three Godfathers, She Wore a Yellow Ribbon, Rio Grande,* and *The Searchers*. During this time, they also produced *The Quiet Man,* released in 1952, a sentimental tale set in Ireland. In the short run, when first shown in theaters, all of these films delighted audiences and proved successful at the box office. In the long run, as film critics continued to study and reevaluate them over the years, they came to be seen as classics of the American cinema. Film historian Ephraim Katz singles out the Westerns, saying:

> [They] betray a deep sense of nostalgia for the American past and the spirit of the frontier. Ford was a folk artist, a master storyteller, and a poet of the moving image. His [camera] compositions have a classic strength in which masses of people and rock formations are beautifully juxtaposed, often in breathtaking

Wayne plays Lieutenant Colonel Kirby York in John Ford's movie *Rio Grande* (1950), the third movie in Ford's trilogy, about the commanding officer of an isolated post, whose enlisted son shows up to prove himself to his father.

long shots. The movement of men and horses in his Westerns has rarely been surpassed for regal serenity and evocative power.

The thought that he might be making a classic that future film historians would analyze did not occur to Wayne, however, when Ford summoned him to star in *Fort Apache* in 1948. The actor was just glad to be working again with the director who had not only a reputation as one of the best filmmakers in the world but also an uncanny ability to bring out the best in Wayne himself. It was Ford, after all, who had coached the actor to what critics at the time still considered his two best performances—in *Stagecoach* and *The Long Voyage Home*. Wayne felt that working with Ford was more than a chance to make money and appear in a first-rate film. It was also an opportunity to continue learning his trade and to grow as an actor.

Wayne was well aware that the benefits of working with Ford the genius came at a price. Ford the director was known for being moody, temperamental, and a highly demanding perfectionist. On his sets, he was a petty dictator who often scolded, yelled at, patronized, and played tricks on his actors, including Wayne, whose star status did not afford him any special rank in Ford's eyes. Any actors or technicians who objected to Ford's gruff style soon found themselves blacklisted from his films, so most learned to take what he dished out and keep their mouths shut. This was often no easy task, as Wayne learned on the *Stagecoach* set when the director arrogantly took the credit for discovering Monument Valley, the magnificent scenic location with the towering stone spires and mesas that came to be the trademark of the great Ford Westerns. Wayne had come across the spot while working on a Western in the early 1930s. "For ten years I held that back as a possible future location," the actor later recalled:

Finally when John Ford decided to use me for a lead in *Stagecoach,* he said, "Now if I could only find a fresh picturesque area to represent the West of the 1800s." I promptly suggested Monument Valley. He promptly suggested that I was hired as an actor and not as a director; but he took note of what I had said and upon his return from location hunting, I was standing with some of the crew when he approached, and said, "I have found the most colorful location that can ever be used for a picture." Then he looked directly at me and said, "Monument Valley." And I assure you from that moment on . . . Ford discovered Monument Valley.

Director John Ford is seen here making a movie in Monument Valley, Arizona, in 1946. Ford claimed *he* discovered Monument Valley as the ideal location for a Western; the towering stone spires and mesas came to be the trademark of the majestic Ford Westerns.

For Wayne, though, Ford's ability to get effective performances from actors more than made up for his

In *Fort Apache,* the first film of John Ford's Western trilogy, Wayne (kneeling at center) was reunited with actor and friend Ward Bond (behind Wayne at right). The critics lauded Wayne's solid performance in the 1948 action-packed cavalry picture.

eccentric and irritating personality. And Wayne found his expectations amply rewarded; his performance in *Fort Apache* was considered, by critics and fans alike, one of his best. He played a captain in a frontier cavalry outpost who must put up with the arrogance and incompetence of a new commanding officer, portrayed convincingly by Henry Fonda. When the commanding officer orders a foolhardy and unsuccessful attack on a band of Indians, an incident in which he dies and Wayne's character escapes, the captain shows compassion and nobility by

covering up for the commanding officer, a man he despised. Critics gave the film high marks and many singled out Wayne in particular. The *New York Times*'s esteemed critic Bosley Crowther wrote, "John Wayne is powerful, forthright, and exquisitely brave."

The critics were also kind to Wayne when his next collaboration with Ford, *Three Godfathers,* reached theaters in 1949. Joining him in the cast were his friends Ward Bond and Harry Carey, Jr., who had appeared in other Ford films. In fact, Ford tended to use many of the same lead and character actors repeatedly, especially in his Westerns, and the group often went by the nickname of the "John Ford rolling stock company." *Three Godfathers* recounts the story of three tough bank robbers fleeing after a heist. In the desert they find an infant whose parents have recently died and end up caring for and protecting the child at the risk of their own capture. Again, audiences and critics praised both Ford's direction and Wayne's performance. Howard Barnes of the *New York Herald Tribune* called the actor "better than ever as the leader of the badmen," and Bosley Crowther said Wayne was "wonderfully raw and ructious [full of rustic humor]."

Wayne and Ford realized that they had stumbled upon a screen formula that worked—namely, Ford's expertise at telling a Western story combined with Wayne's unique mixture of macho strength and gruff sentimentality. So they continued to collaborate on Westerns, turning out *She Wore a Yellow Ribbon* and *Rio Grande* in rapid succession in 1949 and 1950. Wayne again played cavalrymen in these films, which completed what became known as Ford's cavalry trilogy, begun with *Fort Apache.* The actor was 42 years old when shooting began on *Yellow Ribbon* and he and Ford decided to stretch his acting range a bit by having him portray an older character—a graying officer on the verge of a reluctant retire-

In the film of the same name, the Three God-fathers—Pedro Roca Fuerte (Pedro Armendariz), Robert Marmaduke Hightower (Wayne), and William Kearney, "The Abilene Kid" (Harry Carey, Jr.)—take charge of a newborn, who they bravely try to save during a perilous journey to the nearest town.

ment. The part proved to be a superb vehicle for Wayne. One critic hailed his performance, saying, "Mr. Wayne, his hair streaked with silver and wearing a dashing mustache, is the absolute image and ideal of the legendary cavalryman."

In 1952, Wayne played another aging character, this time a retired American boxer who settles in Ireland and woos an Irish woman, in *The Quiet Man,* the only non-Western he and Ford made during this period. Describing the romantic comedy and Wayne's performance, biographer Alan Barbour states:

Combining pastoral beauty with the sort of rowdy Irish comedy Ford always favored in his films, *The Quiet Man* delighted movie audiences. . . . [An] important ingredient in the success of the film was the breathtaking color photography which forever captured on film the exhilarating beauty of the countryside. [Cinematographer] Winton Hoch added another Academy Award to the one he received for *She Wore a Yellow Ribbon*. Ford, who often touted *The Quiet Man* as one of his favorite films, was similarly honored when the Academy gave him its Oscar as best director of the year. It was his sixth such honor. Wayne demonstrated that he was able to handle a delicately shaded and complex role with consummate skill and understanding.

Wayne's consistently good reviews in Ford's films helped keep the actor in the box office top 10 year after year. He was also able to command the then astronomical salary of half a million dollars per picture by 1954. One way Wayne exercised his growing power in the business was to form his own production company in 1954, naming it Batjac Productions after the Batjack Trading Company in his 1949 adventure film *Wake of the Red Witch*. His immediate goal was for Batjac to make pictures with moderate budgets that would turn a modest profit and build up his credibility as a producer. Because he could make more money working for other companies than he could afford to pay himself on his own films, he acted in only one of the early Batjac productions—*Blood Alley* with Lauren Bacall.

Another reason Wayne did not involve himself heavily as an actor in his own company's projects was that he wanted to remain free to take good roles for important directors when the opportunities arose. Certainly, playing any role John Ford had to offer him took precedence over all others. Although he did other films during these years, notably action pictures such as *Flying Leathernecks* in 1951 and *Big Jim McLain* in 1952, both he and the public knew that his best work remained the movies on which he collaborated with Ford.

71

Wayne's next chance to work with Ford did not come until more than three years after the release of *The Quiet Man,* but for Wayne the wait turned out to be worth it. Ford asked Wayne to play a character named Ethan Edwards in an unusually dramatic and colorful Western titled *The Searchers.* Marking the zenith of the Wayne-Ford collaboration, the film has since been widely acclaimed as one of the two or three greatest American Westerns, and many critics consider Wayne's work in the picture his all-time best.

Adapted by screenwriter Frank S. Nugent from a novel by Alan LeMay, the story of *The Searchers* begins when Edwards, a tough and introverted loner, returns to his brother's farm in the desert Southwest at the close of the Civil War. Shortly after his arrival, while Edwards is away for the day, his brother and most of his family are massacred by renegade Indians. The Indians kidnap Edwards's two nieces, and he and a family friend spend the next five years searching for the missing girls. Eventually, they find that one of the girls has been killed, the other indoctrinated into tribal society. Edwards, who has a blind and deep-seated hatred for Indians, is torn between killing his surviving niece, in his eyes now little more than an animal, and completing his long and lonely mission of rescuing her. At the crucial moment, Edwards overcomes his own prejudice and saves her.

Wayne saw the part of Ethan Edwards as the most challenging of his career. As written by Nugent, it was a role of enormous power and complexity—a loner who feels as alienated from the white society that sired him as from the Indians he hates, a man racked by bitterness over the fact that the woman he loved married his own brother and who finds himself called upon to save the daughter of that union. Wayne felt sure he could capture Edwards's lonely spirit but counted on Ford to help give the character depth and texture. Although he had received good reviews for Ford's films, Wayne had often been cited by critics as being more of a personality than an actor. He was quite sensitive to the charge frequently leveled at him—that "John Wayne knows only how to play John Wayne"—and was eager to prove he was capable of portraying characters with depth.

In *The Searchers,* as in some of their earlier films together, Ford's ability to bring out Wayne's best qualities proved crucial. In particular, Ford was adept at making an actor's character appear to mesh perfectly with his or her own personality and public image, creating the illusion that no one else could do the role justice.

Ethan Edwards (Wayne), wounded, writes his will in John Ford's masterpiece *The Searchers* (1956). According to critic James Monaco *The Searchers* was "a critical breakthrough for Ford, Wayne, and the genre. The Traditional Western hero and the Cavalry [are] shown in an unusually critical light."

According to film historian Stuart M. Kaminsky in his book *American Film Genres:*

> In a Ford film . . . there is a tacit assumption that the individual actor is reflecting an essential part of himself in the film role, that he is the type of character that he portrays. In actual fact, as far as Ford's principal characters are concerned, the character can have radical differences from the actor; but Ford is always careful to play on the viewer's basic expectations of an actor. . . . This is . . . true, for example, of the characters John Wayne has played in such films as *Stagecoach, The Long Voyage Home, She Wore a Yellow Ribbon,* and *The Searchers.*

Indeed, in shaping Edwards's character, Wayne and Ford played on viewers' expectations of John Wayne as a strong, silent, macho hero who could be counted on in a crisis. In these respects, Wayne and Edwards were the same. But beneath the surface lurked darker, more uncertain aspects of the character—feelings of bitterness, uncertainty, loneliness, and fear of loving what he is conditioned to hate. The actor and director succeeded in showing these more antiheroic qualities of the character in subtle yet dramatic ways. One of the most touching examples is the scene near the beginning of the film in which Edwards and his brother's wife find themselves momentarily alone in the farmhouse living room. They do not speak, and in fact their eyes hardly meet, yet their suppressed feelings of unrequited love for each other are subtly apparent in their body movements. Wayne again underplays with great dramatic effect in the film's finale. After giving up years of his life in search of his niece and having returned her to white society, he, a loner who feels uncomfortable among his own kind, wanders away unthanked and unnoticed. It is one of American cinema's most moving moments.

To understand why Wayne receives substantially more acclaim for his role in *The Searchers* today than he did when the film was first released in 1956, one must remember that often his pictures that were released back-to-back varied enormously in quality and that the mediocre ones tended to detract from the good ones. Ironically, 1956 was the year in which his very best and worst films opened in theaters. Most people who loved him in *The Searchers* that year thought he appeared

In 1956, Wayne, surrounded by autograph seekers, tries to make his way toward the theater for the premiere of his film *The Conqueror* in Berlin, Germany. The movie, about the life of the Mongol conqueror Genghis Khan, is considered to be the worst of Wayne's films.

ridiculous in *The Conqueror,* a horrendous biography of the menacing Mongol, Genghis Khan. Wayne was anything but menacing in the film, however. He not only seemed totally miscast in the costume epic but also had trouble making the script's many awkward and poorly written lines sound convincing. One of the most famous, or perhaps infamous, examples was a line directed at his leading lady and spoken in his customary Western drawl—"Yer beau-ta-ful in yer wrath." Wayne was out of his element and he knew it. "It's small wonder that he got drunk on the set of *The Conqueror,*" Shepherd and Slatzer comment. "Given the circumstances, it took great courage for him to sober up at all during the filming of that picture."

As it turned out, Wayne had other reasons for wanting to forget about *The Conqueror.* Years later, many of the actors and technicians who worked on the film, including Wayne, contracted cancer. The proportion of cast and crew who got the disease was so much higher than what is considered typical for a random group of individuals that some survivors suspected that the film's shooting location was a contributing factor. Much of the filming took place in a stretch of Utah desert in which the government had tested atomic bombs only two or three years before. Whether or not lingering radiation took its toll on an unsuspecting Hollywood crew remains uncertain. But eventually seeing so many of those who had worked on *The Conqueror* dying around him was surely a constant reminder to Wayne of one of the low points of his life.

Wayne preferred to remember the high points of his career and he later looked back fondly on the remarkable creative output his films with John Ford constituted. Perhaps Wayne began to sense what critics and audiences already knew in their hearts—that the Wayne-Ford classic Westerns would live on to thrill new generations, that they would become symbols of the old West, in their own way just as immortal as the Monument Valley vistas in which they were created. Certainly, Wayne's likeness as a Western hero will always be associated with these vistas. In a very real sense, in making *Fort Apache, The Searchers,* and his other mythic Westerns, Ford added a new monument to the valley—the timeless celluloid image of John Wayne in Western garb and riding a horse.

⑥ Remembering the Alamo

FOR MUCH OF HIS ADULT LIFE, John Wayne had dreamed of making his own film about the Alamo. The 1836 siege in which 187 Texans made a brave but futile stand against an army of nearly 5,000 Mexican troops under General Santa Anna fascinated and inspired Wayne. He identified with the Americans who settled Texas, then a Mexican province, in the 1820s and 1830s. When the Mexican government demanded that they conform to Mexican laws and customs, the settlers refused, provoking Santa Anna's attack on the 187 Texans, who used an old San Antonio church called the Alamo as a fort. To Wayne the dramatic 13-day siege, in which the Americans, including frontier heroes Jim Bowie and Davy Crockett, died to the last man, was one of the great symbols of American valor and freedom. He believed that audiences shared his feelings enough that they would flock to theaters to see a large-scale film depiction. After a long period of scrambling to raise the capital to make the film, Wayne launched preproduction for *The Alamo* in 1957 and the project literally consumed his life until the picture's release in 1960. Although audiences and critics did not receive it in

Wayne directs a scene in the film epic *The Alamo* in November 1959. The movie preoccupied Wayne for more than three years, and although it was not a hit at the box office, it fulfilled his longtime dream and made a noble statement of his patriotic beliefs.

79

quite the way he had hoped, completion of the film fulfilled his longtime dream and constituted a majestic expression of his patriotic beliefs and values. And his participation as producer-director-star was by far the largest single example of all-around artistic output in his long career.

Exactly when Wayne first began dreaming about bringing the Alamo story to the screen is hard to determine. It might have been as early as the 1930s when he was still churning out B Westerns, although at that point it is doubtful that he envisioned he would ever have the stature in Hollywood to produce and direct such a project. By the late 1940s he felt he did have such standing and approached the head of Republic Pictures about an Alamo film.

Unlike most would-be producers, who approached potential backers with visions of making money and besting other producers and studios, Wayne expressed patriotic reasons for wanting to do the project. He summed up his feelings in a later press release, saying:

> I hope that seeing the Battle of the Alamo will remind Americans that liberty and freedom don't come cheap. I hope our children will get a sense of our glorious past, and appreciate the struggle our ancestors made for the precious freedoms we now enjoy—and sometimes just kind of take for granted.

The cool reception Wayne received at Republic was repeated numerous times in the early 1950s. By this time the so-called cold war with the Soviet Union was of major concern to Americans, especially conservative ones like Wayne, and the actor felt more than ever that the nation needed the patriotic boost an Alamo film could provide. "The growing defeatist attitude in the Cold War imposed on us by the Soviet [sic] is a disgrace," he said. "They are trying to defeat us by breaking our spirit and morale.

America—the true, legendary, heroic America—fears no bullying nation." Wayne stressed that a film about the Alamo would show the world "the sort of spirit and indomitable will for freedom that I think still dominates the thinking of Americans." But his attempts to raise the necessary money for the project, which he planned to direct rather than star in, constantly failed. Most studios liked the concept of an Alamo movie. But Wayne's idealism was simply not enough for the hard-nosed, dollars-and-cents-minded Hollywood money brokers. They had to be sure such a film would be profitable, and that meant signing up appropriate big-name stars and an experienced, proven director. As Shepherd and Slatzer explained:

> The biggest problem he faced was in getting major-studio distribution. Most studios saw potential in a film based on the battle of the Alamo; most thought it good business to employ the nation's top box-office draw; and most were willing—some even expressed eagerness—to produce such an epic. To ensure the film's financial success, all wanted Duke to star in the picture and none wanted him to direct it. Duke was a movie star, not a director, and the thought of giving him a multimillion-dollar epic for a learning experience seemed an absurdity to them.

But the film was Wayne's personal dream, his "baby," and he felt that his producing and directing it was the only way to ensure it would make it to the screen the way he envisioned it. So year after year he continued to push the project, using his influence as a top box office star in every way he could. Finally, in 1957 he managed to strike a deal with United Artists (UA), which agreed to put up $2,500,000 for the project and allow Wayne to direct on two conditions. First, Wayne's own company, Batjac, which would produce the film, would have to match UA's investment dollar for dollar. Second, Wayne would have to star in the picture, in order to boost its potential

Wayne portrays Colonel Davy Crockett in the recreation of the 1836 battle at the Alamo. In order to make a deal with United Artists (UA) to help finance the *Alamo* project, Wayne had to agree to match UA's offer dollar for dollar and star in the movie.

at the box office. Wayne realized that he might never again get so serious and acceptable an offer from a major studio and he signed the deal.

With his dream project at last seemingly a reality, Wayne immersed himself in the preproduction aspects of the project. It was an enormous undertaking, especially

82

because he demanded that everything about it be as spectacular and authentic as possible. His art director, Alfred Ybarra, faithfully reproduced the Alamo mission itself after closely studying the original, which still stands today as a tourist attraction in downtown San Antonio, Texas. The film's re-creation of 1830s San Antonio, along with the mission replica, was erected on a 400-acre sight Wayne leased in Brackettville, Texas, about 120 miles west of the actual historic location. Of course, the usual procedure in reproducing western towns for films was to construct realistic-looking but inexpensive false building fronts. However, Wayne and his crew went considerably further. He later remembered:

> When we first went down [to Brackettville], we planned to use ordinary false-front sets for the town and the shell of the Alamo. Then we figured the cost of trailers to house actors and crew and got around to the idea of putting up buildings instead. We put dressing rooms in some build-ings, used others for warehouses. So we came up with something we hadn't intended, and before we got through we'd built a town.

The construction of real buildings for the San Antonio sets, which cost an estimated $1 million—a huge sum for a single film set today let alone in the late 1950s—was only one of Wayne's lavish expenditures. According to Aissa Wayne,

> [The film's initial budget] was about $7.5 million, remark-ably high for those times. Determined to make a film that would endure, my father spared no expense for precise authenticity. . . . He hired 5,000 cast members to ensure that war scenes would look like actual battles, not the same 100 men shot at fifty different angles [a common Holly-wood trick]. Temporary housing had to be constructed. And as I recall, stars and extras alike got to dine on thick Texas steak and lean roast beef. The morale on the *Alamo* set was soaring.

Five thousand of Santa Anna's troops attacked the Alamo, which was defended by 187 Americans and Texans. In Wayne's film, the Alamo was authentically re-created at a cost of about $1.5 million.

The budget for the film was also soaring, however. When the initial money was spent, Wayne had to raise more. He got some of what he needed from a group of Texas businessmen, then mortgaged Batjac, his own house, and

even the family cars. "I have everything I own in this picture," he told the press, "except my necktie."

After more than two years of research, planning, hiring, construction, traveling back and forth between California and Texas, and scraping for money, John Wayne's monumental Alamo project was ready to go before the cameras. On September 22, 1959, the 321 crew and principal cast members assembled in the re-created version of San Antonio in Brackettville. Among the actors were the popular stars Richard Widmark, who would portray Jim Bowie, Laurence Harvey as Colonel Travis, the Alamo commander, and Richard Boone as General Sam Houston. Wayne cast himself in the pivotal role of frontiersman Davy Crockett. Wayne's daughter Aissa and son Patrick had small roles in the film and his eldest son Michael, who was 25, worked behind the scenes as associate producer, basically as the producer-director's all-around assistant.

The filming went smoothly, particularly considering that Wayne was a first-time director helming a picture of gigantic proportions. But he had been thinking about and planning for this shoot for years and when the fateful time for execution came he ran cast and crew through their paces in a competent and professional manner. Many on the set were especially impressed with how well Wayne and his actor friend Jack Pennick organized and staged the huge battle scenes that highlighted the last quarter of the film. All through the shooting, whatever skill Wayne might have lacked as a director he made up for in determination, hard work, and relentless attention to every detail of production. When the 84 days of shooting wrapped on December 15, 1959, the director-star pronounced himself satisfied that he had done his best. It was now up to the public to judge if his best was good enough.

Indeed, public reaction to *The Alamo* was crucial to its success, and the film's publicist, Russell Birdwell, who had worked in that capacity on the legendary movie *Gone with the Wind,* went immediately to work on promotion. He released a huge 173-page packet of information about the film to the press and also sent the material to newspaper columnists, government officials, libraries, and schools. Birdwell and Wayne also stirred up a bit of controversy by combining the promotion with political rhetoric in a $152,000, three-page ad in the July 4, 1960, edition of *Life* magazine. The ad, which pictured a half-demolished Alamo, suggested that, although Crockett, Bowie, and the other Alamo heroes were true Americans who died for their convictions, the candidates running for president of the United States in 1960—John F. Kennedy and Richard M. Nixon—might have few convictions of their own. "Who has written his speeches?" the ad asked about Kennedy:

> Who—or what board of ghostwriting strategists—has fashioned the phrases, molded the thoughts, designed the delivery, authored the image? . . . Who is the actor reading the script?

> There were no ghostwriters at the Alamo. Only men.

Many more ads and promotions led up to the official opening of the film at the Woodlawn Theater in San Antonio on October 24, 1960. The spectacular premiere included a visit from the governor of Texas, an international press conference, a parade featuring a gigantic cake shaped like the Alamo, a Mexican-style fiesta, and a concert in which Dimitri Tiomkin, composer of the film's dramatic and moving music score, conducted "The Alamo Suite." At the time of the premiere, the film ran for 3 hours and 12 minutes and included an intermission. However, the distributor cut out about half an hour of footage before releasing the picture to theaters around the country.

Accompanying *The Alamo*'s general release, of course, were the important critical reviews that could potentially help or hurt the film's box office success. Wayne was disappointed by the lukewarm reception most critics gave his frontier extravaganza. *Newsweek* magazine said of the

---

film, "Its own place in history will probably be that of the most lavish B picture ever made . . . 'B' for banal." And *Time* magazine stated, "*The Alamo* is the biggest Western ever made. Wayne and company have not quite managed to make it the worst." Most other important reviews echoed these, although many critics praised the film's

While on the set of *The Alamo*, Wayne and his daughter, Aissa, who acted a part in the film, unwrap chewing gum. Wayne's film, which was originally 192 minutes long but was cut down to 140 minutes, cost Batjac Productions more than $15 million to make.

photography, attention to authenticity, and especially Wayne's exciting staging of the battle scenes. Though his pride was hurt, Wayne took the negative press in stride. He was confident that the industry itself would prove the critics wrong by honoring the film with Academy Awards and that the picture's stirring subject matter would motivate the public to ignore the reviews and flock to the theaters.

In fact, to Wayne's delight, his pet project received a formidable six Oscar nominations. These were for best sound, best song, best color cinematography, best music score, best supporting actor—for veteran character actor Chill Wills—and best film. Although somewhat disappointed at not receiving a nod as best director, Wayne took comfort in the best-film nomination, which was an acknowledgment of his overall work as producer. Unfortunately, he and Birdwell were so anxious to promote the movie to the Academy voters that they went a bit overboard in their ads in the trade newspapers. The suggestion seemed to be that voting for *The Alamo* was the patriotic and "American" thing to do. "This is not the first time the Alamo has been the underdog," Wayne told *Variety.* "We need defenders today just as they did 125 years ago."

Many people in the business were offended by Wayne's ads and a few said so publicly. Dick Williams, an editor for the Los Angeles *Mirror,* wrote:

> The members of the Academy . . . are being subjected to one of the most persistent pressure campaigns this year I have seen since I started covering the Oscar show 13 years ago. . . . The implication is unmistakable. Oscar voters are being appealed to on a patriotic basis. . . . This is grossly unfair. Obviously, one can be the most ardent of American patriots and still think *The Alamo* was a mediocre movie. . . . Wayne obviously takes his own advertisements seriously. I wonder how many other Academy voters will also?

Perhaps Wayne began to realize that he had gone too far when actor Chill Wills started placing his own similar but even more outrageous ads promoting his best-supporting-actor nomination. Alongside a picture of the film's cast standing in front of the real Alamo, Wills printed, "We of *The Alamo* cast are praying harder—than the real Texans prayed for their lives in the Alamo—for Chill Wills to win the Oscar." Like nearly everyone else in Hollywood, Wayne thought Wills's ads were in poor taste and publicly disavowed any connection with them. Wayne hoped that the controversial atmosphere surrounding the Oscar race would not alienate the Academy voters and hurt *The Alamo*'s chances.

Whether the Academy voters did indeed feel alienated or whether they just felt the other nominees were better is impossible to say. Whatever the reason, Wayne's film won only one Oscar—for best sound. And this disappointment was followed by another. Whereas Wayne had counted on a good showing at the box office, the film grossed only $8 million in its first year of release, less than it had cost him to make. Not only did he lose his own Batjac investment, but in order to pay back his private backers he sold his interest in the project to United Artists. The studio later made a decent profit on the picture thanks to grosses from worldwide distribution but it was too late for Wayne to cash in.

Despite his disappointments, Wayne was not defeated by the experience. He was still a big star with substantial earning power, he knew, and would in time be able to get back on his financial feet. And he really seemed to feel that all the hard work and learning time spent behind the camera had made him a better person. As his daughter Aissa so aptly put it:

Although my father toiled on it on and off for ten years, and it drove him to the financial brink, I never heard him complain about how things turned out. . . . I think my father was always a dreamer. I believe it's one of the reasons he loved making Westerns, where he could get out under the stars and be boyish again, riding horses and shooting guns and playing cowboy. For all the heartache and lost money it must have caused him, I think [he] understood that he'd given his *Alamo* dream his very best shot, and that this in itself made him a winner.

7 An American Hero Versus the Two Big Cs

THE PERIOD OF THE 1960s was a turbulent one for John Wayne. He had lost a great deal of money on *The Alamo* and needed to keep working steadily to stay financially solvent. But this was not as easy for him as it had been in his younger days, when lining up work meant simply finding roles that called for a rough and tough leading man. He was now in his fifties and faced the necessity of creating a new, older screen image that would still be attractive and acceptable to audiences.

As the years wore on, he began to experience other reminders that he was getting older. Several of his lifelong friends, some barely older than he, became ill and died. And he had his own frightening bouts with cancer, first lung cancer, which he called the "big C," a battle he courageously fought and won, and later, cancer of the lymph system, to which he eventually succumbed. Also, the older he became, the more the world seemed to change around him, often in ways that worried and frustrated him. In particular, he worried about the worldwide spread of communism, which he believed posed a grave threat to democracy and freedom, a threat he felt too many Americans took

---

In the 1969 Western *True Grit* Wayne plays U.S. Marshal Rooster Cogburn, a man of "true grit" who agrees to track down a murderer in Indian territory. Wayne won an Oscar for his performance.

extremely lightly. For Wayne, communism represented another "big C" that needed to be fought and eradicated.

Wayne's battle against communism had begun several years earlier. As the cold war with the Soviets began in the late 1940s, he, along with many other Americans, became convinced that the Communists were engaged in a conspiracy to destroy the world's democracies and install Communist dictatorships in their places. Wayne was a conservative Republican obsessed with the idea of maintaining traditional American values, chief among these being freedom of speech, action, assembly, and worship. In his view, the "Commie bastards," as he called them, wanted to take these rights away and they were steadily infiltrating American society in an ongoing attempt to destroy it. One main target of the Communist conspiracy, Wayne and others held, was the entertainment business, which had a strong influence in shaping social opinions and values.

Worried about Communists infiltrating the film industry, in 1948 Wayne joined and became president of the Motion Picture Alliance for the Preservation of American Ideals, a group with the goal of rooting out Communists in Hollywood. Among the alliance's prestigious members were Wayne's friends Ward Bond and John Ford, and Clark Gable, Ronald Reagan, Gary Cooper, Robert Taylor, and Adolphe Menjou. The main function of the alliance was to report the names and suspicious activities of Hollywood actors, writers, directors, and technicians to the House Un-American Activities Committee (HUAC; a special committee formed in 1938 by the U.S. House of Representatives to investigate alleged Communists whose activities were considered a threat to American democracy). This government group held public hearings in which it questioned, embarrassed, accused, and in effect condemned many people suspected of being Communists. Thanks to the work of the alliance and HUAC, hundreds of members of the film industry, many of them innocent, were blacklisted, or barred from getting work, in the 1940s and 1950s.

By the early 1960s HUAC had been discredited as a witch hunt, as un-American as those it perceived as the enemy, and with the return of more liberal attitudes in Hollywood the alliance had largely fallen apart. It was precisely this "softening" attitude toward communism that Wayne objected to. He believed that the Communists were as big a threat as ever and he did not, as some of his colleagues had, apologize for his earlier work in the alliance. Wayne stated:

> Our organization was just a group of motion-picture people on the right side, not leftists and not Commies. . . . When Congress passed some laws making it possible to take a stand against these people, we were asked about Communists in the industry. So we gave them the facts as we knew them. That's all. The only thing our side did that was anywhere near blacklisting was just running a lot of people out of the business.

Those of his colleagues who disagreed with Wayne pointed out that "running people out of the business" and blacklisting were pretty much the same thing. His apparent conviction that making it impossible for politically suspect people to work in their chosen field was acceptable behavior was an example of a darker, meaner side of Wayne that usually only family, friends, and associates knew about. For instance, although he displayed a warm, friendly, and laid-back demeanor most of the time, he was prone to occasional vicious outbursts of temper when things did not go his way. According to Aissa Wayne:

> As a child I saw him rage at other people on his film sets. It was awful to witness. Though he never cursed at his family, when my father yelled at adults he peppered his

speech with obscenities. I'd cringe and hold my breath until it was over, a tightness inside my throat. I never saw him put his hands on anyone, but he was a powerful man, and I knew he could hurt someone if he chose to.

It is likely that Wayne's continued public stand against communism in the 1960s was another way he chose to vent his anger. He had never hesitated to openly denounce political or social ideas and institutions he found irritating, offensive, or dangerous and made no exception in the case of communism. In fact, he seemed to feel it was his patriotic duty to use his fame and position in the film industry in any way he could to aid the anticommunist cause. Perhaps the most obvious example was the way he chose to support the Vietnam War in the mid-1960s. He believed that protest against the war undermined the efforts of the American soldiers and that the honorable thing to do was to back them up in every way and bring

Colonel Kirby (Wayne) of the Green Berets leads his men during a battle in Vietnam. *The Green Berets,* released in 1968, immortalizes the elite combat troops who fought the Communists during the Vietnam War.

the conflict to a quick and decisive end. "If we're going to send even one man to die," he declared, "we ought to make it an all-out conflict."

For his part in that conflict, in 1968 Wayne marshaled the forces of Batjac Productions to make *The Green Berets,* a patriotic war drama about an elite group of combat troops vanquishing sinister Communists in Vietnam. Wayne played the group's leader and also directed the film. Strictly in a filmic sense, *Berets* was a well-made action piece. But most people on both sides of the political fence were more interested in the way the film shamelessly promoted the views of John Wayne, who for many had become one of the chief spokespeople for American superpatriotism. Not surprisingly, the movie sparked controversy. As Alan Barbour explained:

> [*Berets*] made those who supported his views quite happy and those who opposed literally livid with anger. When the film was released, there were pickets lined up outside many of the theaters. Congressmen, mostly confirmed "doves" regarding the war, made waves in the Senate, claiming that Wayne had used American men and property [some U.S. soldiers had helped in the filming] to express a slanted viewpoint of the way things really were overseas.

As he usually did when people criticized his political views, Wayne largely ignored the controversy over *The Green Berets.* But other distressing aspects of his life were more difficult to ignore. In the early 1960s, several of his closest friends died, including actor Gary Cooper, a companion from the alliance, and Wayne's publicist, Beverly Barnette. Perhaps the death that hit Wayne the hardest was that of Ward Bond, not only his costar in many films but also an old football and drinking buddy. Bond was only two years older than Wayne and his death from a heart attack forced Wayne to consider the fact of his own advancing age.

Wayne also directed *The Green Berets*, which his son Michael produced. Although most people believed it was a well-made action movie, the film was criticized for espousing Wayne's political views.

Like it or not, Wayne realized, he was now in his fifties and looked it. He reasoned correctly that audiences would no longer find him believable as the young, athletic leading man, who at the end of each picture wins the love of the young, buxom leading lady. Yet he was still good-looking and vigorous. And his screen presence remained strong and commanding. It seemed logical, then, to choose roles that mirrored the conflict he faced in his own personal life—that of wrestling with and to a measurable degree overcoming the inevitable effects of growing older. His first film role of the 1960s, in *North to Alaska* with Stewart Granger, another aging leading man, firmly established Wayne's new image. He played a middle-aged gold miner who is very much set in his ways, does not trust women, and, like Wayne himself, resists but eventually must give in to and accept change. In coming to grips with the realities of growing old, the character recognizes and sees the humor in his own shortcomings. According to Shepherd and Slatzer:

> In many respects, his new image was a re-creation of himself, set in fictional worlds where the lines between good and evil, right and wrong were clearly defined and widely separated. It was this new image that firmly established him as a national institution and an ageless international superstar and that eventually won him an Academy Award. It was the John Wayne image, the one by which he would come to be identified and remembered the world over.

In the films that followed, including *The Comancheros* (1961), *The Man Who Shot Liberty Valance* (1962), *Hatari!* (1962), and *McLintock!* (1963), Wayne reaffirmed his new, aging, but still magnetic image.

Wayne's career adjustment had allowed him successfully, if temporarily, to deal with the outward aspects of growing old. But he soon found himself besieged by an inward and much more serious aspect—that of declining health. The first ominous signs appeared when he was in the midst of shooting *In Harm's Way,* a World War II drama, in the summer of 1964. A cough that had been bothering him for almost a year worsened to the point that it interfered with his delivery of lines. He suspected that it was related to his smoking habit—three to five packs a day since the 1930s—a potential hazard he had not taken seriously before. After a 1962 interview with Wayne, author Dean Jennings wrote:

> As he talked, frequently cussing and using the same grim drawl that has cowed badmen from Fort Dodge to Tombstone, he compulsively lighted one cigarette after another. "So maybe it's six months off the end of my life," he said, opening the day's fifth pack, "but they're not going to kill me."

The actor stubbornly stuck to this naive belief in spite of his persistent and painful cough on the set of *In Harm's Way*. Convinced that it was nothing serious, he took cough syrup and refused to see a doctor.

Eventually, as the cough continued to worsen, Pilar insisted that her husband get a medical checkup. Wayne later recalled his confrontation with a radiologist after undergoing a series of X rays, a brief but dramatic interchange that might have come from the script of one of his movies:

> "I already had a chest X ray taken a few months ago for *Harm's Way*," Wayne said.
>
> "Yes, I know," replied the other man. "We have it."
>
> "Then why all these X rays?"
>
> "We're trying to determine how far it's gone."
>
> "How far *what's* gone?" asked Wayne. "You mean I've got cancer?"
>
> "Yes," came the solemn answer. "You have cancer."

Wayne had a large tumor—in his own words, "the size of a baby's fist"—in his left lung and the doctors gave him only 1 chance in 20 of surviving. But he was determined to beat the disease and approached the surgery on September 16, 1964, with the same brand of courage displayed by some of the most stalwart of his screen

In February 1966, Wayne and his wife, Pilar, hold newborn daughter, Marisa Carmela, at their home in Newport Beach, California. Wayne had heroically survived surgery for lung cancer two years earlier.

characters. The doctors managed to remove all traces of the tumor, but soon after the operation, his whole body began to swell alarmingly. Wayne had to undergo another surgical procedure only six days later to reverse the life-threatening condition.

Fellow actors help Wayne celebrate his 40th anniversary in films in 1969. From left to right are Lee Marvin, Clint Eastwood, Rock Hudson, Fred MacMurray, John Wayne, James Stewart, Ernest Borgnine, Michael Caine, and Laurence Harvey.

The doctors were amazed enough that the actor had survived both the cancer and the second grueling operation. They were simply flabbergasted when Wayne, who in their opinion needed at least 6 months for a full recovery, was back on his feet in only 3 weeks and at work on a new movie just 14 weeks after the surgeries. Wayne, minus his cigarettes, reported to the set of a Western, *The Sons of Katie Elder,* in January 1965. Reporters who

visited him on the set walked away with the impression that he was bigger than life offscreen as well as onscreen. He had grappled with the "big C," he told them, and won.

Wayne proved to be a winner in a different way as the most turbulent decade of his life drew to a close. In 1968 he received an offer to play an aging, one-eyed deputy marshal named Reuben J. "Rooster" Cogburn in a film

based on Charles Portis's novel *True Grit*. Wayne found himself fascinated by and drawn to a kind of role he had never before considered, that of a dishonest, unkempt, and in many ways thoroughly unappealing individual. He later recalled, "Rooster was the kind of marshal never portrayed on screen before: an old, sloppy-looking, disreputable, one-eyed sonofabitch who used every trick, fair or foul, to get his man. And that's the way I played him." Wayne's broad portrayal of Rooster as a lumbering, ornery, pathetically comical old man wearing an eye patch certainly constituted a marked departure from his earlier screen roles. Yet, just as he had expected, audiences loved the character as much as he did.

On April 7, 1970, Wayne wipes away a tear after singer and actress Barbra Streisand handed him the 1969 Academy Award for best actor for his performance in *True Grit.*

To Wayne's surprise, many people in the film industry liked his performance, too. First he received the Golden Globe Award as best actor, and then came the news that he had been nominated for an Oscar, his first such nomination since *Sands of Iwo Jima* in 1949. Despite being up against stiff competition—Dustin Hoffman and Jon Voight in *Midnight Cowboy,* Peter O'Toole in *The Lion in Winter,* and Richard Burton in *Anne of the Thousand Days,* Wayne won. When singer-actress Barbra Streisand opened the envelope and announced his name, John Wayne, his eyes welling up with tears, strode to the podium in what was perhaps the proudest moment of his career. "Wow!" he declared in his world-famous drawl:

> If I'd known that, I'd have put that patch on thirty-five years earlier. Ladies and gentlemen, I'm no stranger to this

podium. I've come up here and picked up these beautiful golden men before, but always for friends. One night I picked up two: one for Admiral John Ford and one for our beloved Gary Cooper. I was very clever and witty that night—the envy of, even, Bob Hope. But tonight I don't feel very clever, very witty. I feel very grateful, very humble, and I owe thanks to many, many people. I want to thank the members of the Academy. To all you people who are watching on television, thank you for taking such a warm interest in our glorious industry. Good night.

According to close family members, another aspect of the *True Grit* experience was just as important to Wayne as winning the Oscar. He had always claimed that he did not care what the critics said about his acting, but the truth was that bad or unkind reviews hurt him a great deal. So he was particularly proud and happy about his rave notices for his portrayal of Rooster. The one that always remained his favorite was by film critic Andrew Sarris of *The Village Voice,* who wrote shortly after the film's release, "There is talk of an Oscar for Wayne after forty years of movie acting and after thirty years of damned good movie acting."

8 ★ The Genuine Article

N HIS LAST YEARS, as his health rapidly deteriorated, John Wayne fought a heroic battle to stay alive. He also fought to keep working, but found that he had in some ways become a dinosaur, a throwback to an earlier age of moviemaking. The industry had changed, largely not to his liking, and good roles for him became increasingly scarce. Ironically, his last role, that of a dying Western gunfighter, closely mirrored his own loss of health, sadness about growing old, and nostalgia for a legendary past, a bygone film age of which he himself remained a living symbol.

For more than a decade Wayne had been observing and complaining about changes both in the way movies were made and how they appeared onscreen. In particular, he did not like the trend, begun in the 1950s and 1960s, of portraying male leads with major psychological and social handicaps and problems. He felt that a movie hero should be a solid, stable, completely masculine type whom audiences could look up to and admire. So the more modern, complex, and realistic depiction of weaker, less admi-

---

In *The Shootist,* Wayne's final film, he portrays J. B. Brooks, a legendary gunfighter who valiantly, but unsuccessfully, battles against cancer. The character's dramatic fight against ill health paralleled Wayne's own struggle with cancer.

rable men—exemplified by Marlon Brando in *A Street-car Named Desire,* Montgomery Clift in *Suddenly, Last Summer,* and Dustin Hoffman in *Midnight Cowboy*—bothered him. Wayne said,

> Ten or fifteen years ago, audiences went to pictures to see men behaving like men. Today there are too many neurotic roles. . . . A lot of writers go far afield to find American men who are extreme cases. They aren't representative of the average man in this country, but they give the impression that we are a nation of weaklings who can't keep up with the pressures of modern living.

By the early 1970s, Wayne discovered that the old-fashioned kind of roles that interested and suited him were increasingly hard to find.

Wayne also disliked other aspects of the new movie realism. For example, he believed that sexual themes and images were better left to the imagination. Also, he was against the graphic depiction of blood on the screen. He was not averse to showing violence, for he had certainly contributed more than his own share of fistfights, shoot-outs, and other kinds of mayhem to film lore. However, showing the actual bloody results of such violence seemed to him unnecessary and disgusting. But eventually, and reluctantly, he had to bow to the pressures of a changing business. During the filming of *The Cowboys* in 1971, the time came to record the violent fight scene between Wayne's character, a cattleman in charge of a group of school-age cowboys, and the villain, played by actor Bruce Dern. The director insisted that the two participants in the fight be made up with appropriate cuts, bruises, and blood effects. But Wayne's makeup man and friend, Dave Grayson, was reluctant. "I can do it if Duke permits me to," Grayson told the director. "But it'll take four makeup men."

"Why four makeup men?" the director asked.

"Three are gonna have to hold him down," answered Grayson.

Grayson had the unenviable task of telling Wayne what the director wanted. At first the actor resisted the idea. "You know I don't believe in that stuff," he told Grayson. But Wayne was a practical man and realized that no matter what he thought about it, audiences now expected to see such realism. So he finally gave in, provided the filmmakers refrained from extremely graphic effects, like "bodies opening up and liver flying out at you." This small but symbolic concession to changing times was difficult for the actor and, as was his habit, he tried to cover up his discomfort with a bit of humor. Upon seeing his bloodied image in a mirror at the end of the makeup session, he quipped, "For crissakes, why don't you put a little *more* blood on me?"

Wayne had to contend with changes in his private life, too. By the early 1970s, his constant preoccupation with his film work and long periods away from home, factors that had contributed to the breakdown of his first two marriages, had taken their toll on his third. Pilar and he had grown apart, and they finally separated in November 1973. Wayne did not find himself lacking female companionship, however. He had recently formed a close relationship with his new secretary, Pat Stacy, who was 34 years younger than he. A warm, caring individual who sincerely loved Wayne, she remained steadfastly at his side in the following years as his health began to fail.

That Wayne was not feeling his usual self became increasingly obvious to friends and coworkers in 1974 during the shooting of *Rooster Cogburn,* in which he portrayed the character he had made famous in *True Grit.* He was irritable, cantankerous, and more temperamental than ever on the set and only Pat Stacy and his costar, the gracious and diplomatic Katharine Hepburn, seemed able to calm him and bring out his good side. Wayne

In 1974, Katharine Hepburn (right) costarred with Wayne in *Rooster Cogburn*. She later remarked that Wayne had "A face alive with humor . . . and a sharp wit."

deeply respected Hepburn, with whom he had never worked before, and in the short time they knew each other she grew equally fond of him. Describing him in a later interview, she said, "A face alive with humor . . . and a sharp wit. Dangerous when roused. . . . Funny. Outrageous. Spoiled. Self-indulgent. Tough. Full of charm. Knows it. Uses it. Disregards it."

Wayne, who now more than ever projected the image of a hard, gruff, no-nonsense character, occasionally revealed unexpected flashes of his warmth and humor to the public, too. In 1974 he received a letter from the editor of the *Harvard Lampoon,* the Cambridge, Massachusetts–based left-wing student humor publication noted for satirizing various American people and institutions. The editor wrote:

> We've heard you're supposed to be some kind of legend. Everybody talks about your he-man prowess, your pistol-packing, rifle-toting, frontier-taming, cattle-demeaning talents, your unsurpassed greatness in the guts department. . . . You think you're tough? You're not so tough.

The editor called Wayne the "biggest fraud in history" and challenged him to come to Cambridge, "the most hostile territory on earth." With a grin, Wayne told Stacy, "I'm going to give those young bastards the goddamndest surprise of their lives."

Wayne accepted the challenge. Obligingly helping the students poke fun at him, he rode into Harvard Square atop a 13-ton army personnel carrier before a screaming crowd of more than 2,000 people. Then he faced a throng of students in a packed Cambridge theater and deftly fielded a barrage of outrageous questions. "Where did you get that phony toupee?" one student dared to ask. "It's not phony," Wayne drawled. "It's real hair. Of course, it's not mine, but it's real." The audience burst into laughter and applause.

The questions and Wayne's rapid-fire, glib answers continued. Q: "What are your views on women's lib?" A: "I think they have a right to work anyplace they want to . . . as long as they have dinner on the table when you come home." Q: "Has President Nixon ever given you suggestions for your movies?" A: "No, they've all been successful." Q: "Is it true that since you've lost weight,

A bugler announces the arrival of Wayne, atop an army tank, in Harvard Square, in Cambridge, Massachusetts, in 1974. Wayne amiably accepted the *Harvard Lampoon*'s challenge to face the students' criticisms and questions.

your horse's hernia has cleared up?" A: "No, he died and we canned him, which is what you are eating at the Harvard Club." Wayne quickly earned the respect of the *Lampoon* crowd, who honored him with the Brass Balls Award for "outstanding machismo and a penchant for punching people in the mouth." The actor phoned Stacy that night to say he'd had one of the most enjoyable times of his life.

But such pleasant experiences had clearly become the exception to the rule. Wayne was even more irritable and hard to work with in 1975 on the set of *The Shootist* than he had been on *Rooster Cogburn.* He had screaming matches and tense verbal exchanges with the director and many members of the crew, and it was clear to those who knew him that something was seriously wrong. Dave Grayson suspected his friend might have heart trouble.

And this turned out to be the case, for doctors eventually diagnosed a defective heart valve. When making *The Shootist,* the story of an aging, dying gunfighter who must come to grips with his own mortality, Wayne had no idea it would be his last film or that the ensuing events of his own life would parallel those of the character he played in it.

Early in 1978, Wayne underwent heart surgery at Massachusetts General Hospital. Although his operation was a success and he seemed like his old self for a while, he found that his health problems had only just begun. He soon developed hepatitis and had to stay in bed for six weeks. Then he began having acute stomach pains and the doctors suspected his gall bladder. In time, they found that he had cancer of the stomach and they removed that organ entirely, replacing it with a new one fashioned from part of his upper intestine.

More bad news followed the surgery. The cancer had spread to his lymph system and further operations would be useless. While undergoing the only potentially effective treatment available—radiation—in February 1979, Wayne found that although he could again eat solid foods he was too nauseous most of the time to do so and he continued to lose weight. His physical appearance deteriorated so badly that when Dave Grayson showed up in Los Angeles to make him up for the yearly Academy Awards show, Grayson was stunned and saddened. According to Shepherd and Slatzer:

> Duke was waiting for him, seated in a chair without his shirt or toupee. Nothing . . . could have prepared him [Grayson] for what he saw. He was shocked but tried not to show it. Duke laughed. . . . "I thought I'd shock you," he said. . . . Duke was pale and had wasted away to half his chest size. . . . His face had shrunk to half its normal size, too. . . . Duke hadn't lost his sense of humor. As Grayson opened his makeup case, Duke looked at himself in the mirror and said jokingly, "I'm looking so damn good, Dave, I don't think I need any makeup."

All made up and wearing his tuxedo, Wayne was a frail but genial and distinguished figure that night at the Oscar ceremony. When he appeared onstage to present an award, the audience gave him a sincere standing ovation. Clearly touched by the gesture, he said:

> That's just about the only medicine a fellow would ever need. Believe me when I tell you I'm mighty pleased that I can amble down here tonight. Oscar and I have something in common. Oscar came to the Hollywood scene in 1928. So did I. We're both a little weatherbeaten, but we're still here and plan to be around a whole lot longer.

Wayne meant what he said. Despite his seemingly hopeless condition, he desperately wanted to live and apparently believed that he might manage again to defeat his old nemesis, the "big C," to cheat death one more time. He had expressed that belief in a March 1979 interview with television journalist, Barbara Walters. "Off-camera, off-screen," she asked, "do you like you?"

"I'm crazy about me," he replied. "I just want to be around for a long time."

"At this point in your life, having faced illness—I guess having faced the prospect of death . . . do you have a point of view that you think kind of sums up your thinking today?"

"The fact that He [God] has let me stick around a little longer," said Wayne, "or *She's* let me stick around . . . certainly goes great with me, and I want to hang around as long as I'm healthy and not in anybody's way."

"Do you fear death?" she asked pointedly.

His answer was very direct. "I don't look forward to it, because, you know . . . maybe He isn't the kind of father that I've been to my children. Maybe He's a little different; maybe He won't be as nice to me as I think He will. But I think He will."

"Stick around for a while longer," said Walters.

"I sure want to," he said.

But this was one fight that John Wayne could not win and the interview with Walters turned out to be his last. His illness and the side effects of the radiation grew worse and he became progressively weaker. Because the radiation treatments had not worked, the doctors tried stimulating his immune system with chemicals but that also proved futile. During the last few weeks of his life a number of friends and well-wishers paid him brief visits. Among them were actor James Stewart, singer Frank Sinatra, and President Jimmy Carter, who supported a U.S. Senate bill to issue a special gold medal in his honor. On the obverse, or front, of the medal was Wayne's portrait, with the inscription: "John Wayne, American"; the reverse side showed an

On April 9, 1979, three months after his cancer surgery and two months before his death, John Wayne jokes with photographers at the 51st annual Academy Awards ceremony in Los Angeles. When he approached the stage to present an award, the audience welcomed him with a heartfelt standing ovation.

image of Monument Valley, which he had helped to immortalize.

Wayne was extremely proud when told about the medal but did not live to see its issue. Finally bedridden, he fell into a coma on June 8, 1979. When he suddenly regained consciousness the next night, Pat Stacy and all his children were at his bedside and he joked and watched television with them for a while. After a few hours, he slipped back into the coma and came out of it only once more, for a few minutes on the morning of June 11. When Stacy asked if he recognized her, he replied, "Of course I know who you are. You're my girl. I love you." These were his last words. That afternoon, surrounded by his children, he died at the age of 72.

All across the United States, tributes to the fallen star attempted to sum up his legacy to the film industry and to the American people. Perhaps President Jimmy Carter, who, despite the vast differences in their political views, greatly admired Wayne, best explained why the actor was so appealing to and beloved by so many millions of people. "He was bigger than life," Carter said. "In an age of few heroes, he was the genuine article. But he was more than a hero; he was a symbol of many of the qualities that made America great. The ruggedness, the tough independence, the sense of personal courage—on and off screen—reflected the best of our national character."

Appendix ★★★★★★★★★★★★★★★★★★★★

A SELECTED FILMOGRAPHY

In all, John Wayne appeared in 153 feature films. Some of the earliest of these were pictures made in the 1920s in which he played minor roles such as students and football players. Many others were B Westerns turned out in only a few days or weeks each in the 1930s. Wayne's more important and better-known films, along with pertinent information on each, are listed here.

THE BIG TRAIL (1930)
Director: Raoul Walsh.
Cast: John Wayne, Marguerite Churchill, Tully Marshall. Wayne's first leading role after being discovered by Walsh; a big-budget Western notable for its panoramic vistas of the old West.

STAGE COACH (1939)
Director: John Ford.
Cast: John Wayne, Claire Trevor, Thomas Mitchell. The film that made Wayne a star; now considered one of the classic Hollywood Westerns.

THE LONG VOYAGE HOME (1940)
Director: John Ford.
Cast: John Wayne, Thomas Mitchell, Barry Fitzgerald. Wayne plays a Swedish sailor in what both he and the critics considered one of his best performances.

REAP THE WILD WIND (1942)
Director: Cecil B. DeMille.
Cast: John Wayne, Ray Milland, Paulette Goddard. A spectacular sea adventure featuring a fight with a giant squid in the finale.

FLYING TIGERS (1942)
Director: David Miller.
Cast: John Wayne, John Carroll, Anna Lee. Wayne pilots war planes in this World War II drama.

BACK TO BATAAN (1945)
Director: Edward Dmytryk.
Cast: John Wayne, Anthony Quinn, Richard Loo. Wayne is part of the heroic anti-Japanese Philippine resistance in World War II.

THEY WERE EXPENDABLE (1945)
Director: John Ford.
Cast: John Wayne, Robert Montgomery, Donna Reed. In still another war saga, Wayne portrays a torpedo boat commander.

ANGEL AND THE BADMAN (1947)
Director: James Edward Grant.
Cast: John Wayne, Gail Russell, Harry Carey. Wayne is a tough gunfighter who meets his match in the form of a pretty young Quaker woman.

FORT APACHE (1948)
Director: John Ford.

Cast: John Wayne, Henry Fonda, Shirley Temple, Ward Bond. The first part of Ford's classic "cavalry trilogy," with Wayne squaring off against his post commander, played convincingly by Fonda.

RED RIVER (1948)
Director: Howard Hawks.
Cast: John Wayne, Montgomery Clift, Joanne Dru. In this classic Western, Wayne delivers one of his best performances as a gruff cattleman.

THREE GODFATHERS (1949)
Director: John Ford.
Cast: John Wayne, Harry Carey, Jr., Ward Bond. Wayne plays one of three bank robbers who, during a sandstorm, find a woman in labor. After giving birth, the dying woman asks the three men to save her baby.

SHE WORE A YELLOW RIBBON (1949)
Director: John Ford.
Cast: John Wayne, Joanne Dru, John Agar. In this second installment of Ford's "cavalry trilogy," Wayne is effective as an aging career officer who is forced to retire.

SANDS OF IWO JIMA (1950)
Director: Allan Dwan.
Cast: John Wayne, John Agar, Forrest Tucker. Wayne won his first Oscar nomination for his portrayal of a tough marine sergeant.

RIO GRANDE (1950)
Director: John Ford.
Cast: John Wayne, Maureen O'Hara, Ben Johnson. In the last part of Ford's renowned trilogy, Wayne plays a commanding officer whose son reports for duty at the remote army post.

THE QUIET MAN (1952)
Director: John Ford.
Cast: John Wayne, Maureen O'Hara, Barry Fitzgerald. Wayne is an ex-boxer who travels to Ireland in one of his and Ford's best films.

THE HIGH AND THE MIGHTY (1954)
Director: William A. Wellman.
Cast: John Wayne, Claire Trevor, Robert Stack. Wayne is forceful as an airline pilot who must use all his knowledge, wits, and courage to keep his plane from crashing.

THE CONQUEROR (1956)
Director: Dick Powell.
Cast: John Wayne, Susan Hayward, Pedro Armendariz. Believe it or not, Wayne as Genghis Khan. A horrid film and perhaps the actor's worst performance.

THE SEARCHERS (1956)
Director: John Ford.
Cast: John Wayne, Jeffrey Hunter, Natalie Wood. Wayne gives perhaps his finest performance in this gripping Western, considered by many critics to be one of the greatest American films.

LEGEND OF THE LOST (1957)
Director: Henry Hathaway.
Cast: John Wayne, Sophia Loren, Rossano Brazzi. Wayne finds a city buried in the Sahara Desert in this modern-day adventure tale.

THE BARBARIAN AND THE GEISHA (1958) *Director:* John Huston.
Cast: John Wayne, Eiko Ando, Sam Jaffe. Wayne portrays an American diplomat assigned to Japan who falls in love with a native woman.

RIO BRAVO (1959)
Director: Howard Hawks.
Cast: John Wayne, Dean Martin, Walter Brennan, Ricky Nelson, Angie Dickinson. In this entertaining film, Wayne plays a tough western sheriff who battles an evil cattle baron.

THE HORSE SOLDIERS (1959)
Director: John Ford.
Cast: John Wayne, William Holden, Constance Towers. Wayne delivers a competent performance as a Union commander who is sent on a daring raid in Confederate territory.

THE ALAMO (1960)
Director: John Wayne.
Cast: John Wayne, Richard Widmark, Laurence Harvey. Wayne plays Colonel Davy Crockett in this spectacular rendition of the legendary battle. Wayne's directing, though far from inspired, is admirable considering the scope of the production and the fact that the film represented his first directing experience.

NORTH TO ALASKA (1960)
Director: Henry Hathaway.
Cast: John Wayne, Stewart Granger, Ernie Kovacs. Wayne is a gold miner in this entertaining comedy-adventure.

THE MAN WHO SHOT LIBERTY VALANCE (1962)
Director: John Ford.
Cast: John Wayne, James Stewart, Lee Marvin. In this interesting, offbeat Western, Wayne, who plays a rancher, gives one of his better performances.

HATARI! (1962)
Director: Howard Hawks.
Cast: John Wayne, Hardy Kruger, Red Buttons. Wayne plays a big-game hunter in Africa.

DONOVAN'S REEF (1963)
    Director: John Ford.
    Cast: John Wayne, Lee Marvin,
    Elizabeth Allen. Wayne is a
    former navy officer who buys
    a bar on a South Sea island.

CIRCUS WORLD (1964)
    Director: Henry Hathaway.
    Cast: John Wayne, Claudia
    Cardinale, Rita Hayworth.
    Wayne portrays the owner of
    a circus that experiences a variety
    of problems and perils.

THE SONS OF KATIE ELDER (1965)
    Director: Henry Hathaway.
    Cast: John Wayne, Dean Martin,
    Martha Hyer. Wayne is a
    gunfighter who returns to his
    mother's home after her death
    and confronts his siblings.

THE WAR WAGON (1967)
    Director: Burt Kennedy.
    Cast: John Wayne, Kirk Douglas,
    Howard Keel. A gold miner
    wrongly jailed, Wayne fights
    against corrupt lawmen.

THE GREEN BERETS (1968)
    Director: John Wayne.
    Cast: John Wayne, David Janssen,
    Jim Hutton. Wayne leads a group
    of special-forces fighters in this
    patriotic Vietnam War drama.

TRUE GRIT (1969)
    Director: Henry Hathaway.
    Cast: John Wayne, Glen
Campbell, Kim Darby. Wayne
won his first and only Oscar
for his performance as the
cantankerous old lawman,
Rooster Cogburn.

THE UNDEFEATED (1969)
    Director: Andrew V. McLaglen.
    Cast: John Wayne, Rock
    Hudson, Lee Meriwether.
    Wayne, a former Union officer,
    becomes friends with a former
    Confederate officer.

RIO LOBO (1970)
    Director: Howard Hawks.
    Cast: John Wayne, Jennifer
    O'Neill, Jack Elam. Once again,
    Wayne is cast as a former Union
    officer, this time getting revenge
    on a gang of outlaws.

THE COWBOYS (1972)
    Director: Mark Rydell.
    Cast: John Wayne, Roscoe
    Lee Browne, Bruce Dern.
    Wayne as an old cattle rancher
    who must take a group of
    inexperienced boys on a
    dangerous cattle drive; one
    of the few times Wayne dies
    onscreen.

MCQ (1974)
    Director: John Sturges.
    Cast: John Wayne, Eddie Albert,
    Diana Muldaur. Wayne plays a
    tough modern-day cop.

ROOSTER COGBURN (1975)
Director: Stuart Millar.
Cast: John Wayne, Katharine
Hepburn, Richard Jordan.
Wayne reprises his role as the
one-eyed rascal, Rooster; his
scenes with Hepburn are
memorable.

THE SHOOTIST (1976)
Director: Don Siegel.
Cast: John Wayne, Lauren Bacall,
Ron Howard. In his last film
performance, Wayne effectively
(and ironically) portrays a
legendary gunfighter dying
of cancer.

Further Reading ★ ★ ★ ★ ★ ★ ★ ★ ★ ★ ★ ★ ★ ★

Barbour, Alan G. *John Wayne*. New York: Pyramid, 1974.

Baxter, John. *Hollywood in the Thirties*. New York: Barnes, 1968.

Everson, William K. *A Pictorial History of the Western Film*. Secaucus, NJ: Citadel Press, 1969.

Kaminsky, Stuart M. *American Film Genres*. New York: Dell, 1974.

Katz, Ephraim. *The Film Encyclopedia*. New York: Crowell, 1979.

The New York Times Film Reviews, 1913–1968. New York: New York Times and Arno Press, 1970.

Shepherd, Donald, and Robert Slatzer. *Duke: The Life and Times of John Wayne*. Garden City, NY: Doubleday, 1985.

Stacy, Pat, and Beverly Linet. *Duke: A Love Story, An Intimate Memoir of John Wayne's Last Years*. New York: Atheneum, 1983.

Walsh, Raoul. *Each Man in His Time: The Life Story of a Director*. New York: Farrar, Straus and Giroux, 1974.

Wayne, Aissa. *John Wayne, My Father*. New York: Random House, 1991.

Chronology ★ ★ ★ ★ ★ ★ ★ ★ ★ ★ ★ ★ ★ ★ ★ ★ ★

1907	Born Marion Robert "Michael" Morrison to Mary and Clyde Morrison in Winterset, Iowa
1910	Morrison family moves to Earlham, Iowa
1916	The Morrisons relocate to Glendale, California, where Marion earns the nickname Duke
1921	Duke enters Glendale High School
1925	Duke is admitted to the University of Southern California on a football scholarship
1926	Mary and Clyde Morrison divorce
1927	Duke becomes assistant prop man at Fox Film Corporation
1929–30	Discovered by director Raoul Walsh and stars in *The Big Trail;* begins using screen name John Wayne
1931	Signs up with the Leo Morrison Agency, signs a contract with Mascot Pictures, and makes the serial *Shadow of the Eagle*
1933	Marries Josephine "Josie" Saenz
1934	First son, Michael, is born
1936	Makes *The Sea Spoilers* and *Winds of the Wasteland;* daughter Toni is born
1939	Director John Ford casts Wayne in *Stagecoach* and Wayne becomes a star; Wayne's son Patrick is born
1940	Josie Wayne gives birth to a daughter, Melinda
1942	Wayne stars in *Reap the Wild Wind* for Cecil B. DeMille
1945	Josie and John divorce in December
1946	Wayne marries Mexican actress Esperanza "Chata" Morrison on January 17
1948	Stars in *Red River* and *Fort Apache;* becomes president of the Motion Picture Alliance for the Preservation of American Ideals

1952	Acts in *The Quiet Man,* directed by John Ford
1953	Divorces Chata in October
1954	Marries Peruvian Pilar Palette Weldy in November
1956	Stars in *The Searchers,* considered by many to be his best performance; daughter Aissa is born
1957–60	Produces, directs, and stars in *The Alamo*
1962	Acts in *The Man Who Shot Liberty Valance* and *Hatari!*; son John is born
1964	Undergoes cancer surgery
1966	Daughter Marisa is born
1968	Directs and stars in the controversial Vietnam War drama *The Green Berets*
1969	Wins best-actor Oscar for *True Grit*
1971	Stars in *The Cowboys*
1973	Divorces Pilar
1976	*The Shootist,* Wayne's last film, is released
1978	Undergoes open-heart surgery
1979	John Wayne dies of cancer on June 11

Index ★★★★★★★★★★★★★★★★★★★★★★★★

Alamo, The (film), 79–91, 93
Allegheny Uprising (film), 54
American Film Genres
(Kaminsky), *74*
Arizona (film), 40

Bacall, Lauren, 71
Back to Bataan (film), 57
Batjac Productions, 71, 81,
84, 90, 97
Big Jim McLain (film), 71
Big Stampede, The (film), 43
Big Trail, The (film), 11–21,
35, 39, 40, 41
Blood Alley (film), 71
B movies, 37, 39, 40, 41,
43, 44, 46, 47, 51, 80,
88
Bond, Ward, 60, 69, 94, 97

Canutt, Yakima, 41, 44, 45,
46, 52
Canutt-Wayne Pass System,
45
Carradine, John, 52
Columbia Pictures, 39, 40
Comancheros, The (film), 99
Conqueror, The (film), 76
Cooper, Gary, 11, 37, 47, 94,
97, 105
Cowboys, The (film), 108

Dark Command, The (film),
54
Deceiver, The (film), 40
DeMille, Cecil B., 54, 55
*Duke: The Life and Times
of John Wayne* (Shepherd
and Slatzer), 13, 16, 25,
40, 44, 56, 76, 81, 99,
114

Feldman, Charles K., 53, 62

Fighting Seabees, The (film),
57
Flying Leathernecks (film), 71
Flying Tigers (film), 56
Fonda, Henry, 68
Ford, John, 47, 48–53, 54,
56, 63, 65–77, 94, 105
Fort Apache (film), 65, 66,
68–69, 77
Fox Film Corporation, 11,
12, 20, 34, 39

Girls Demand Excitement
(film), *39*
Glendale, California, 12, 25
Green Berets, The (film), 97

Hangman's House (film), 34,
48
Harlow, Jean, 40
Harvard Lampoon, 111, 112
Hatari! (film), 99
Haunted Gold (film), 43
Hepburn, Katherine, 109–10
House Un-American
Activities Committee
(HUAC), 94–95
Hurricane Express, The
(serial), 42

I Cover the War (film), 46
Idol of the Crowds (film), 46
In Harm's Way (film), 99, 100

King of the Pecos (film), 46
Kingston, Al, 40, 41

Lady and Gent (film), 43
Lady from Louisiana (film), 54
Lawless Frontier, The (film),
43
Lawless Range, The (film), 46
Levine, Nat, 41

Lonely Trail, The (film), 46
Lone Star Pictures, 43, 44, 45,
46
Long Voyage Home, The
(film), *54, 63, 66, 74*

McLintock! (film), 99
Maker of Men (film), 40
*Man Who Shot Liberty
Valance, The* (film), 99
Mix, Tom, 11, 13
Morrison, Clyde (father),
23–26, 32
Morrison, Marion. *See*
Wayne, John
Morrison, Mary (mother)
23–25, 32
Morrison, Robert (brother),
23, 32
Motion Picture Alliance for
the Preservation of Ameri-
can Ideals, 94–95

North to Alaska (film), 99

Paramount Pictures, 43

Quiet Man, The (film), 65,
70–71, 72

Range Feud (film), 40
Reagan, Ronald, 94
Reap the Wild Wind (film),
54–55
Red River (film), 62
Republic Pictures, 46, 53, 54,
62, 80
Reunion in France (film), 57
Ride Him Cowboy (film), 43
Riders of Destiny (film), 43, 45
Rio Grande (film), 65, 69
Rooster Cogburn (film), 109,
113

Sands of Iwo Jima (film), 59, 104
Searchers, The (film), 65, 72–74, 77
Sea Spoilers, The (film), 46
Seven Sinners (film), 54
Shadow of the Eagle (serial), 41
She Wore a Yellow Ribbon (film), *65, 69–70, 71, 74*
Shootist, The (film), 113
Sons of Katie Elder, The (film), 102
Stacy, Pat, 109, 111, 112, 116, 117
Stagecoach (film), 48–53, 59, 66–67, 74
Star Packer, The (film), 43

Texas Terror (film), 43
They Were Expendable (film), 63
Three Faces West (film), 54
Three Girls Lost (film), 39
Three Godfathers (film), 65, 69
Tracy, Spencer, 40
True Grit (film), 103–5

United Artists, 54, 81, 90
Universal Pictures, 46, 47, 54
University of Southern California, 12, 30–32, 34, 60

Vietnam War, 96–97

Wake of the Red Witch (film), 71

Walsh, Raoul, 11–17, 34–35, 54
Wayne, Aissa (daughter), 25, 34, 35, 45, 59, 60, 83, 86, 90, 95
Wayne, Esperanza "Chata" Morrison (second wife), 60, 62
Wayne, John
    Academy Award, 99, 104–5
    and *Alamo, The,* 79–91
    birth, 23
    as B movie actor, 37–47, 51
    and cancer, 76, 93, 100–103, 107, 109, 113–15
    Canutt-Wayne Pass System, develops, 45
    childhood, 24–30
    death, 116–17
    as director, 80, 81, 86, 97
    divorces and separations, 51, 59, 109
    education, 12, 27–33
    football career, 12, 17, 26, 29, 30, 31, 32, 33, 34, 40
    films, start in, 11–21, 34–35
    and John Ford films, 47, 48–53, 54, 56, 63, 65–77
    marriages, 43, 51
    name change, 13, 35
    patriotism, 59, 80, 93–97
    as producer, 71, 79–91, 97
    as prop man, 12, 34, 39, 48
    Westerns, 11–21, 34–35, 37, 39, 40, 41, 43–46, 48–49, 51–55, 58, 62, 63, 65–77, 79–91, 99, 102, 103–5, 107, 108–10, 113
    and World War II, 55–59
Wayne, John, Jr. (son), 62
Wayne, Josephine Saenz (first wife), 31, 32, 34, 39, 43, 46, 51, 59, 62
Wayne, Marisa (daughter), 62
Wayne, Melinda (daughter), 56
Wayne, Michael (son), 46, 86
Wayne, Patrick (son), 56, 86
Wayne, Pilar Palette Weldy (third wife), 60–62, 100, 109
Wayne, Toni (daughter), 46
Westward Ho (film), 46
Winds of the Wasteland (film), 46
Winterset, Iowa, 23
Words and Music (film), 34

Don Nardo is an award-winning writer. In addition to articles, screenplays, and teleplays, including work for Warner Brothers and ABC Television, he has published more than 50 books, including *Gravity: The Universal Force, The War of 1812, Anxiety and Phobias, The Extinction of the Dinosaurs, Exercise, Ancient Greece, The Roman Empire, Greek and Roman Theater, The U.S. Congress,* and biographies of Charles Darwin, H. G. Wells, William Lloyd Garrison, Jim Thorpe, and Cleopatra. Mr. Nardo lives with his wife, Christine, on Cape Cod, Massachusetts.

Leeza Gibbons is a reporter for and cohost of the nationally syndicated television program "Entertainment Tonight" and NBC's daily talk show "Leeza." A graduate of the University of South Carolina's School of Journalism, Gibbons joined the on-air staff of "Entertainment Tonight" in 1984 after cohosting WCBS-TV's "Two on the Town" in New York City. Prior to that, she cohosted "PM Magazine" on WFAA-TV in Dallas, Texas, and on KFDM-TV in Beaumont, Texas. Gibbons also hosts the annual "Miss Universe," "Miss U.S.A.," and "Miss Teen U.S.A." pageants, as well as the annual Hollywood Christmas Parade. She is active in a number of charities and has served as the national chairperson for the Spinal Muscular Atrophy Division of the Muscular Dystrophy Association; each September, Gibbons cohosts the National MDA Telethon with Jerry Lewis.